Her Cousin Julia

a Novel

Susan M. Szurek

Chapbook Press

Schuler Books
2660 28th Street SE
Grand Rapids, MI 49512
(616) 942-7330
www.schulerbooks.com

Her Cousin Julia

ISBN 13: 9781957169194

Library of Congress Control Number: 2022917327

Printed in the United States by Chapbook Press.

Also by Susan M. Szurek:

Everstille: A Novel

Everstille's Librarian

Olivia from Everstille

Tomas' Children

Some cause happiness **wherever** they go;

others **whenever** they go.

Oscar Wilde

Prologue   Christmas, 1929

Dinner was finished, dishes were done, leftovers were wrapped and put away, and the family was spread around the house, talking or napping. Rose and Maria were seated in the back room on the two comfortable chairs placed side by side. Rose's feet were resting on a tattered hassock, and she was rubbing her swollen belly while Maria slipped off her shoes and rubbed her ankles one at a time. Her belly was not large because she was only three months pregnant compared to Rose's almost seven-month bump. They sat quietly. Maria took a sip of the ginger tea she had brought into the room.

"Still having some sickness?" asked Rose.

"Some," answered Maria, "but it seems to be better this week. Now I have constant heartburn. This ginger tea does seem to help. Thanks for the advice," and she took another sip.

Rose nodded and they were silent. The women had gone to the same high school and had been in some classes together, but they had not been close friends until Rose started dating, then married Maria's brother, Henry. As sisters-in-law, they formed a camaraderie, and with their growing pregnancies, a rapport. They shared a family, a closeness, and a concern about the recent troubles in the country. They were united and content to spend the holiday together. Maria sipped the tea and sighed. A sudden bout of laughter came from the kitchen, and the women turned and smiled at each other.

"They must be playing Dominos," commented Rose. "I hope they don't argue like they did at Thanksgiving."

Maria nodded, finished her tea, bent down, and set her empty cup on the floor. She rubbed her left foot once more and then her right one. "Have you and Henry talked about names yet?"

"He mentioned a few boy's names, and I have a girl's name in mind, but no, no serious talks yet. Henry says he doesn't care if this is a girl or a boy, but I think he'd like a daughter. How about you and Albert?"

"Not really. Albert did say if we have a boy, he'd like an *Albert, Junior,* but I'm not crazy about that. We'll see. We have a few more months to wait than you do, and I'm sure we'll come up with something appropriate. Obviously, he's thinking about a boy, and I'd like a girl, but whatever it is will be fine. Just think, our children will be cousins! They'll grow up in this family. They'll do things together."

"Well, we'll both have boys or both have girls. Of course, we could have one of each. I hope we have the same because it will be easier to raise them together, don't you think?"

"I guess. Boys would be fun. They could play ball in the summers and snowball and sled during the winters. I'm sure their fathers would enjoy taking them to ball games and such."

Rose smiled, "Boys would be fine, but girls would have a closer relationship, I think. There's a bond they would share. They would be cousins and, I'm sure, best friends. They will be like sisters, *almost sisters*, and that will be fun for them, right?"

"It will be," and Maria smiled and reached over to squeeze Rose's hand. "It really will be. The best of friends!"

Chapter 1   Deciding

No matter how often Julia begged her cousin to kill her, June refused.

"Stop that nonsense," June would say, "There is nothing wrong with you. We are the same age, and you are in better shape than me, and I intend to continue living and enjoying life."

Julia snorted in derision. "Of course you will. You have something to live for. You have children and grandchildren, and a group of friends you visit and work out with, and I have no one. Arnie is dead, and I never had children, and my friends, if you can call them that, are also gone. Moved away. Never call or visit. And the ones who do only do so because they think I'll leave them jewelry or money when I'm dead, which I won't. I'll leave it all to you, June. I'll go to the lawyer and amend my will today if you will kill me tomorrow."

June glanced sideways at her cousin, refusing to answer her, and continued to read her book club's next selection. This was a tired harangue. Julia was being ridiculous again, and she didn't mean what she said. She got into these moods and said the wildest things. Suggested insane ideas. It made June regret the move she had agreed to years ago.

Three years ago, Julia suggested that since they were both widows and aging, they combine their households and move together to the Winchester Senior Complex. It sounded logical and reasonable then. Julia had worked out a plan. She talked and pleaded with June for weeks and weeks, and finally after being worn-down by her cousin who would not let the idea go, June agreed. She knew her children had their own lives and families, and she didn't want to be an obligation to them. When they visited the Winchester Complex, June was impressed by the new townhouse which was large: six rooms, two bathrooms, and a pleasant outdoor space. The monthly HOA assessment took care of the lawn work and snow removal, and except for three to enter the townhouse, there were no stairs to climb. The connecting wall to their neighbor was in the garage so they were never bothered by any noise from Mr. Simmons who was, by nature, a quiet person anyway. The Winchester townhouse was in all respects, perfect.

They moved in. A plethora of groups and activities were available for the residents, and once they settled down, June took full advantage of them. Julia did not. She could have, and did attend a few meetings for various groups, but found the people, as she complained to June, *trite* and *insipid*. Those were her words, and she didn't return a second time to any activities. She stayed in the townhouse, watching television, and complaining to June whenever she was around. June enjoyed the clubs and activities, and Julia's petulance was additional encouragement to continue being active. But on the morning of the current conversation, June was still at home for another hour. She was meeting a friend at the exercise room where they were going to join the new group that was starting: Senior Shape-Up. Julia had refused to go.

"*Senior Shape-Up?* No thanks. A bunch of old ladies flapping their arthritic, fatty arms and legs around! Not for me. Why do you want to go? Who are you getting in shape for? Really June, you have the stupidest ideas."

Julia, for all her non-movement, was in decent shape for a seventy-three-year-old. She had always tended to be on the thin side. June was not thin, and she resented the reference to fatty arms and legs, because hers were. But she knew this was typical of Julia's barbed comments and chose to ignore it. She had dealt with her cousin all her life, and knew her commentaries mandated ignoring.

June's father and Julia's mother had been siblings. The cousins were born a few months apart and lived near each other although in vastly different houses. Julia's mother had married a wealthy man and their house was large and expertly decorated, and the family wanted for nothing. And that was saying something because the cousins were born in 1930, the early days of the Depression. June's family resided in a small apartment. Her father married for love and had trouble holding a job even in the best of economic times, so *want* was a routine visitor. She slept in a miniscule bedroom which was a made-over storage space, and jealously arose as Julia lorded her large room and many toys over her cousin. Julia's mother and June's mother had been classmates in high school, so the two families were together often, and the cousins were routinely in each other's company because they were only children. Given their past and the years together, June thought she should be hardened to Julia's grumpiness and grousing, but it was becoming increasingly difficult to take.

Julia glanced at June and questioned, "Did you call the maintenance office about the bushes in back?" Julia thought the back foliage was overgrown and needed trimming. She wouldn't call herself because June, as her unofficial secretary, was expected to take care of such details, a tacit agreement given the money Julia regularly put out.

However, the bushes had been trimmed just over a month ago, and June knew there was no sense in calling.

"Julia, they were just trimmed and are fine. I'm sure they will be clipped again in the fall," and June closed her book and sighed. She got up to pour the last of the coffee into her coffee cup and looked out the back. It would become warm later, but right now it looked pleasant, and she thought she would sit outside for a bit. Away from Julia.

"Coffee again? I HATE the smell, and after all these years, you should know that. Heat up the water for my tea. Really, June, I think you should drink tea instead. It's actually healthier, and if you avoid the cream you put in your coffee, you would lose some of that fat," and Julia reached over for the remote. It was time for her morning game show. She turned the kitchen's television on, adjusted the sound to LOUD, and proceeded to wind her way through the many channels her subscription money afforded them. June rarely watched anything. She stayed busy with other activities.

Making Julia's tea was a specific, consuming process. While the filtered water heated, June reached into the cupboard to remove the tin of expensive imported loose tea from the Harrington Tea Company and place it on the table in front of Julia along with the specially ordered Manuka honey from New Zealand (said to have special healing properties). A spoon, special tea strainer, and a lovely imported tea cup and saucer, part of the keepsakes Julia had obtained during her Europe visits, were set there also. The thinly sliced fresh lemons arrived on another matching plate, and, once organized, Julia arranged her tea to be seeped for four minutes. No more. No less. She timed everything carefully, then poured the tea, added the swirl of honey, and topped it off with a thin lemon slice. She would stir once with the spoon, set it on the extra plate (it was gauche to place a teaspoon directly on the table), and take a delicate sip of the beverage.

June was used to waiting on her cousin in this way. It was an unspoken agreement because most of the money for the townhome and its furnishings and contents and utility bills and HOA payments and groceries and television cable channels and magazine subscriptions came from Julia whose family and dead husband, Arnie, had been wealthy. June had married for love. Like her father. Financial solvency was one of the reasons she had agreed to the living arrangement with her cousin. She knew her measly pension and small social security check would not cover her monthly bills. She sucked it up and for three years, she and Julia had lived together in the fine town house, affording June a financial freedom she would not have enjoyed otherwise.

"Is there anything else you want? I'm going to sit outside and read until time for the class. Are you sure you don't want to go with me? It would be good for you to get out and see some of the women. They ask about you."

"Humph," replied Julia, "They gossip about me, you mean. I hope you keep your big mouth closed and tell them nothing. No, I won't go, and no, there is nothing else I want just now," and Julia turned up the volume as her game show began. She was busy placing the tea strainer onto the matching plate (teabags were also gauche). She checked the time for exactly four minutes of seeping as she watched the program. June slipped out the lovely French doors which lead from the kitchen to the back, and she seated herself on one of the soft cushioned patio furniture chairs. Julia had ordered them specially made.

She put her coffee cup on the table to her side and opened the book. She had lost interest in reading but needed to get away from her cousin whose penetrating, squawking laughter could be faintly heard through the French doors. June often second-guessed her decision to live with her cousin. It wasn't easy and was becoming more difficult as the years went on. She had been hesitant to make this move, but Julia convinced her. "We'll be fine," Julia explained. "It will be delightful to live together. We have so much in common and know each other so well," she elaborated. "It will all work out." But being tethered to someone because of money was torturous, and the past three years had been particularly grueling.

June looked over the carefully and expertly manicured compact lawn to the impeccably trimmed small bushes. Across the way was the large two-story building which housed Winchester Complex's offices, rental rooms, library, and gym. The large first-floor exercise area was where she would go to flap around her fatty arms and legs and to remove herself from the continuing comments, mostly nasty, of her cousin. Julia had become increasingly curmudgeonly, and at times like these, in the draining, difficult days which were becoming more frequent, June questioned her living arrangement. She was spending increasingly more time reviewing their life together. She spent her time wondering how much more she could take.

Behind her, in the kitchen, she heard Julia yell out incorrect answers to the televised questions and shout at the contestants that they were *dolts* and *idiots*, familiar terms to June. Her book lay open but June was not reading. She was thinking about the conversation from earlier. The one where Julia, once again, bemoaned her fate and her life, although there was nothing to bemoan. The conversation where she asked her cousin to do away with her. It was that conversation and request June was thinking about, deciding about. It would take care and planning and deliberation and more than a smidgeon of fortitude and bravery and luck, but as she stared ahead at the manicured lawn and the bushes that needed no additional trimming; as she listened to the gawking laughter and indelicate language coming from the kitchen, she made a decision. June was going to kill her cousin Julia.

Winchester Senior Complex

Announcing

Senior Shape-Up
New Class

9:30-10:15

Monday, Wednesday, Friday

Come to the Winchester Common
Main Building Exercise Room

Feel Better!

Join your friends for a fun workout!

Wear comfortable clothing and gym shoes.

Chapter 2   1935: Age 5

"Well, my Mama said your mother stole my name and gave it to you." Julia put one hand on her left hip as she held the new doll to her right side with the other hand. She cocked her head to the left and stared at June.

June just looked at her in astonishment. "How can a name be stolen? My name is mine and yours is yours. And my mother doesn't steal anything. Ever! You're wrong!"

The cousins were in Julia's large bedroom looking at the toys Julia received for her fifth birthday. Talk and laughter floated upstairs from the downstairs where adults who had come to celebrate Julia's birthday were gathered. The two girls had been admiring the three new dolls received as birthday gifts. Envy crept into June's soul because the one gift she had received for her birthday some months ago was a small checkers set, and a new doll would have been welcomed. She thought three dolls were an overabundance and hoped Julia would offer to give her one…any one of the three. When she noticed that the *Patsy Ann* doll had a tag that spelled out her name, she mentioned it to her cousin, and the stolen name accusation came up. Julia took her new *Patsy* doll, hugged it, and then repeated what she had recently heard her mother tell a neighbor.

Rose Murray Harris, June's mother, and Maria Harris Reynolds, Julia's mother, knew each other in school but were not particular friends until Rose married Henry Harris, Maria's brother. As sisters-in-law they discovered much in common. That is until Rose stole the name Maria had planned to give her daughter. Their relationship cooled after that. The women expected children within months of each other, and when Rose's daughter was born in March of 1930, she named the little girl *June* after her maternal grandmother. Maria was furious. Her child was due during the month of June and, if a girl, would be named after the month she was born. Such a clever idea, Maria thought as she practiced saying, "This is my daughter, June, born in June." However, Rose got there first, and Maria's daughter, born in the month of June, was given the second-place name of *Julia. (This is my daughter Julia, born in June,* didn't pack the same clever punch.) For a few years, the friendship between Maria and Rose was unsteady. Maria eventually got used to calling the daughter of her brother *June*, but she never completely forgave Rose. Nor did she forget, and the story about the stolen name was periodically told to those who had not heard it.

This was not the first time Julia had tormented June about something she had heard. Just a few months ago, when Julia and her parents had visited June's apartment for an intimate birthday party, the girls were in June's narrow storage area/bedroom, setting up the checker set for a game. As they sat on the bed with the board between them, June captured two of Julia's men and crowned another *King*. Julia stared at the board and then at her cousin. She did not like to be bested, and this was the second game June was winning. It wasn't fair. June should pretend not to see the obvious moves which had taken more of Julia's checkers off the board. She should allow her cousin to win at least once. If she wasn't going to win, then there must be another way to best June. She re-examined the board, looking for the winning move but found none.

Julia lifted hooded eyes to look at her cousin who was examining the board. She thought of something she heard her parents say just the other day, and she repeated it to June.

"My parents said that your family doesn't have a pot to pee in," and Julia repeated almost the exact words she had heard. There was another word used for *pee*, but even she wasn't bold enough to voice it. She waited for June's response.

June looked quizzically at her cousin. She hadn't heard the expression and didn't know its meaning. Of course, neither did Julia, but she would not admit as much.

"What are you talking about?" and June sat up quickly, disturbing some of the checkers which scooted to the right, off their acquired squares. "We don't pee in a pot; we go in the toilet."

"Well, all I know is you don't have the right pee pot," and Julia maintained this invention as she sat up straighter. From across the moving checkers, they looked at each other.

"You know we go in the toilet, because *you* have gone in our toilet." June attempted to set things right. This entire conversation made no sense to her, and she was pretty sure her cousin was making things up. It wouldn't have been the first time. She swung her legs over the side of the bed and put her feet down on the floor, further disturbing the remaining checkers. She stood up straight, facing Julia.

"Come on, let's go to the bathroom now. I'll prove it to you," and June grabbed her cousin's hand and pulled her off the bed as the checkers flopped around on the coverlet. June wasn't sure what was being alleged, but the charge that she and her parents did or did not have the correct pot into which they could or could not place their bodily fluids was so galling that something needed to be proved immediately.

June took Julia's hand and moved her out of the improvised bedroom into the narrow hallway and down into the diminutive but serviceable bathroom where the substantiated pot/toilet could be viewed. As the girls stood at the doorway, the irrefutable proof sat before them, a chip on the seat attesting to its continued use.

"See," and June, probably unnecessarily, pointed to the convenience with righteous indignation. "And we have a washstand and a tub too. You know this."

Julia shrugged. "I just heard that. I don't know. Maybe it means something else. Anyway, I have to pee, so I guess I'll go in. Let's start the checkers game over. OK? Go back and set it up and we'll begin again. We have to because the pieces are knocked down on your bed. I'll be right back," and she went into the disputed room and closed the door.

As Julia shut the door, June stood for a moment wondering if her point had been proven or not. Had she verified her statement? Was their pot/toilet acceptable? It must be if her cousin was using it. She went back to her bedroom, gathered the pieces, and reset the board. As she waited, she wondered again about the aforementioned pot and thought she might ask her parents about it later, but then decided that perhaps the entire issue should be dropped. It was confusing. She replaced the checkers, reset the game, and waited on her side of the board for Julia to reappear.

When the accusation about the stolen name was made at Julia's party, June was unsure how to respond to it. There was no substantial item to point to, like the pot/toilet at her house. Going to the bathroom here, at Julia's house would prove nothing, and the accusation that her mother was a thief, that she would steal anything, was so astounding that June was completely stymied as to what tact to take. So, she said nothing, but decided to completely change the subject. Attacking one's bathroom use and facilities was one thing, but attacking one's parents was completely unethical, and June didn't want to travel this winding amoral road.

"Well, anyway, you are really lucky to get all these dolls. I wish I had a new one. Maybe for Christmas I'll get one," and June patted the *Patsy* doll's soft head and backed out of an argument she wasn't sure how to handle.

"I am lucky. And do you know who gave this to me?" and

without giving June time to answer, she said, "It was my father's Aunt Hazel. You know, the old woman downstairs who has that big lump on her neck. Did you see it?"

The Aunt Hazel who was currently downstairs seated at the dining room table sipping at her tea was the unfortunate recipient of a goiter. Because nothing could be done about it, she was doomed to always keep a shawl or scarf with her, to hide the baseball sized lump away from polite society. However, Julia had seen it in past visits, and she was anxious to show the oddity to her cousin.

"Come on, let's go down stairs and see if we can see her neck. It's really icky, and I dare you to look right at it," and Julia threw the *Patsy* doll back with the others in her collection and grabbed June's hand.

Stolen name business forgotten, they marched down the lovely winding staircase, scurried through the kitchen where Mrs. Sampson, the housekeeper, was directing the hired help as the night's birthday feast was being readied. The girls scooted around the canapes, rolled past the sparkling plates and glasses, maneuvered slowly through the piles of sweets granting them longing looks. They eased their way to the desired objective, through the gathered adults who were talking, holding filled glasses, and ignoring the child with the stolen name whose hand was clutched tightly by the child who had been gifted three additional dolls to add to her growing and totally dismissed collection.

Chapter 3   Justifying

June smiled as she stepped off the scale. She lost three pounds in the last month and was pleased. Her new routine was helping, and she was determined to adhere to it. She and her friend, Alice, loved their *Senior Shape Up* class. Because they enjoyed it so thoroughly, both added *Senior Swim* to their exercise schedule. In the spirit of maintaining a healthy lifestyle, June had decided to skip the daily dessert Julia insisted on and go for an evening walk instead. She asked Julia to walk with her, but Julia refused.

"Walking? Why? There is nowhere I want to go, and I have no desire to run into any of the idiots who live around us. No thanks," and Julia pulled over the rice pudding topped with a mountain of whipped cream, "I'll stay here and watch my game show. Have a good walk!" She reached over to get the remote, found the correct channel, and scooped up an abundant spoonful of the pudding which she deposited into her mouth.

June knew the last comment wasn't sincere, and she dismissed it. She stepped out the French doors onto the deck, walked down the small step into the yard, and took a deep breath. It was late summer, and the weather had been amiable. She thought she would amble along the walking path which circled the man-made lake behind the wooded area. Sometimes she asked Alice to accompany her, but Alice and her husband Wes, were invited to dinner at their daughter's house. June started out across the lawn and towards the green accompanied by nothing but her thoughts.

She allowed her mind to wander to the topic she had been considering for the last weeks: the killing of her cousin, Julia. She was shocked at herself for even thinking such a thing and didn't allow the idea to come back into her mind for a week or so. But slowly, just as slowly as the pounds were easing off her frame, it seeped back. *Kill cousin Julia; Kill cousin Julia*, and now, after three whole weeks, it was there. There was no denying it. When she woke in the morning it was there. When she pulled down the Harrington Tea Company tin and arranged Julia's morning tea, it was there. As she listened to Julia complain about the overgrown (no, they weren't) bushes in the back or the fact that June's coffee smell was "…disgusting, June, simply disgusting!" or that the contestants on the various game shows she watched were brainless and witless, and June's fatty arms were ugly, and her friends, well, former friends, should all go to ...you know where... it was there. The thought was there. Solid and secure. And now, each evening as June walked in lieu of eating dessert, if Alice did not accompany her and talk about the minutia of daily life, the thought of killing her cousin, Julia, was fully and completely ensconced in her prefrontal cortex and her hippocampus, seething, and whirling and waiting for justification. And then action.

Of course, she would never actually do the deed. June was a moral and ethical person, brought up to believe in the precepts of the Presbyterian church. Murder was wrong. It was prohibited in the fifth commandment. Or was it the sixth? The Presbyterian Church did not believe in capital punishment either, and neither did June. Although if someone killed any of her family, shouldn't they be killed in return? And June was almost certain she would be able to press the button or pull the switch or whatever means would be used to murder the murderer who murdered her family member. But this idea about committing murder was nonsense. She chided herself for it. She tried thinking about other things: her book club, her grandchildren, her late husband. But the thought just would not go away.

Tonight, during this walk, she was determined to face the thought (*Kill cousin Julia; Kill cousin Julia*) and erase it from her mind. She would make a mental list of the reasons why she shouldn't/ wouldn't/ couldn't kill her cousin Julia, and force herself think about it. HARD. Then it would be gone. She would create a *Con* list. There would be no *Pro* list because there could not be a reason for one. She would analyze, contemplate, consider, and once this foul thought was eliminated, she would feel *clean* again. She had not felt that way since this dreadful idea crept in, and she needed to rid herself of what she was beginning to think of as a *sin*. Certainly it was according the fifth (sixth?) commandment.

She thought through the reasons killing cousin Julia would be wrong. June formed a blackboard in her head. She mentally wrote the word *Con* on it and then immediately got sidetracked. What did *Con* stand for? Contrary? Contradictory? Converse? She tried to think back to her schooling, but she couldn't remember any teacher had ever explained the meaning of *Pro/Con*. She was sure *Pro* meant...no, she wasn't sure of anything. Prosperous? Proponent? Proposal? Wait, she remembered it might have been a Latin term. She would check it when she returned to the house, but for now she needed to return to the mental blackboard. *Con/Against.*

She created a list, numbering one to five to begin:

1.
2.
3.
4.
5.

She began to write with her magic mind chalk:

CONS

1. Killing is illegal.
2. Killing is unethical.
3.
4.
5.

Then she stopped. She looked down at her shoe. She had stepped in dog poop with both feet, and she almost swore. Must be Mrs. Crenshaw's dog. She never cleaned up the droppings and had been warned about taking her dog on the walking path without cleaning up its messes, and this was an exceedingly large mess. June found a stick and wiped off what she could and then ran the bottom of her shoes along the dried leaves and grass. Great! She could just hear Julia's complaining and yelling about the smell, so she would need to remember to remove her shoes before entering their house. She removed what she could, then resumed her walk and her blackboard.

She was having trouble coming up with another *Con*. Perhaps the two were sufficiently powerful. She thought about adding "Murder is tricky and hard to get away with," but decided that was not rational and not in keeping with the decency of the first two reasons. Anyway, only one of those reasons was sufficient. And weren't they the same? She considered looking up the words *illegal* and *unethical* when she returned home.

June looked ahead at the path. She saw a young couple coming towards her but didn't recognize them. Sometimes, other people came to walk the path along the lake although this was private property belonging to the Winchester owners, but if they were polite and respectful, she didn't mind. Julia did, however. Just a week ago, as they sat in their front room watching the large television, Julia spied a couple pushing a stroller and walking past their window. She denounced their actions. "Who are those people? The police should be called. June, call the main office first and then the police. Unfamiliar people shouldn't be walking in front of my townhouse or anyone's townhouse. I have a mind to go and yell at them." But she didn't. And June didn't call anyone because when she got up to see where they were going, as Julia demanded she do, they turned into the townhouse just down the way. The young couple were relatives of Gemma Anderson and had come for a visit. June informed Julia about this. She replied "Humph!" and mumbled something under her breath about *trespassers*.

As June and the couple passed, they smiled and greeted each other. June was glad Julia hadn't come on this walk. She would have made a scene. She took a deep breath and the passing scent of Mrs. Crenshaw's dog's leavings drifted to her nostrils. She ignored it and went back to her board. She couldn't think of additional *Cons*, and refused to consider *Pros*, but somehow the magic chalk wrote the word PROS on its own, and June allowed her mind to fill in a list.

PROS

    1. Julia is mean.
    2. Julia is cruel.
    3. Julia is unkind.
    4. Julia cheated on her husband. (Pretty sure)
    5. Julia is brutish to animals. (So I heard)
    6. Julia lies.
    7. Julia is uncharitable.
    8. Julia is overbearing, oppressive, domineering....

June stopped walking. She made herself stop thinking about the list. There were other words and reasons which crowded her mind, but she would not allow them in. This was not what she meant to do. She would not, could not justify such an act. What was wrong with her? She felt tears coming to her eyes and took three deep and slow cleansing breaths, just as Doctor Spanner once taught her to do. She looked up and saw she was almost at the end of the path. She finished her walk. *I am going to go home and take a bath and read the Bible. Wonder where it is?* And June purposely walked quicker and got back to the house and opened the French doors. Julia was still seated at the kitchen table watching television.

June forgot to take off her shoes. She walked into the kitchen and as she entered, so did the smell of Mrs. Crenshaw's dog's mess. Immediately Julia yelled. Her olfactory sense was acute and discerning, and she knew that odor.

"What the Hell, June? Are you dragging crap into this house? Did you dirty your pants? What is going on?" and Julia held her nose.

June backed out into the yard, removed both shoes and came back in explaining what happened on her walk. Julia barely listened. She didn't care what happened.

"Just clean this floor. We can't wait for the cleaning woman. Get it done now. Disgusting, disgusting smell. Dogs should be outlawed! And you should be more observant! Really, June, what a sickening thing to drag in! How stupid of you!" and she got up from the chair and moved swiftly and instantly into the front room, settled on her favorite chair, turned on the television, and continued to complain loudly.

June walked over to the closet containing the cleaning supplies, removed the bucket, mop, and special floor cleaning fluid (Julia ordered it from a company which sold organic, essential lemon oil-scented floor cleaning fluid.) and begin her project. The noise from the television almost drowned out Julia's continued complaining as the floor was cleaned, sanitized, disinfected. As June repeatedly and carefully moved the mop back and forth, erasing the odious reminder of her solitary walk, a small repetitive sound formed in the recesses of her brain. The recurrent, persistent refrain sounded: *Kill cousin Julia; Kill cousin Julia; Kill cousin Julia.*

Winchester Senior Complex

Walking Path Rules

Hours: 7:00 am until 9:00 pm

Winchester residents only

No bicycles or motorized vehicles

Keep to the right

Do not litter

Dogs must be leashed

Clean up after your dog

Do not pick any flowers

Enjoy your walk!

Chapter 4   1940 Age 10

Chicago was sharply frigid in December, but neither June nor Julia cared about the weather. They could barely sit still in the back seat of the car as Julia's parents dove into downtown Chicago. They were going to the United Artists Theater to see Walt Disney's new movie *Fantasia,* and then out to dinner at the Hoe Sai Gai Chinese Restaurant where they were excited to eat their dinner using chopsticks. This was June's Christmas gift from her aunt and uncle, and she had been looking forward to it since December 25 when she opened the gift-wrapped box under the tree at Julia's house. When she saw a menu from the restaurant and a rolled-up poster picturing Mickey Mouse in a starry robe with the caption *Walt Disney's Technicolor Feature Triumph:* FANTASIA, she was confused and frankly disappointed. She was expecting a doll or a new game. Her disappointment vanished when Julia's mother, Aunt Maria, explained what it meant.

Julia's father, Uncle Albert, had connections, and with just one phone call, was able to obtain the poster for June (and, of course, one for his own daughter). He sent his secretary over to the Chinese restaurant to get a menu (and an order of their beef chop suey for his lunch), and June's gift was complete. Once she realized that she would be going downtown (she had only been there twice before) to the special movie everyone at school had been talking about (and no one had seen yet), and then out to dinner at a *Chinese* restaurant (first time ever!), she was thrilled and delighted, and hugged Aunt Maria and Uncle Albert, and jumped up and down with Julia as they held hands and chanted "Mickey Mouse, Mickey Mouse." It was her favorite gift that year.

And now it was Friday, December 27, and June's gift had arrived. She was allowed to wear her almost new, olive-green Sunday dress with the white Peter Pan collar and cuffs. Her mother insisted she wear her snow boots instead of her good shoes, even though there was little snow outside, and June gave in after a brief argument because she was too excited to protest further. She stood at the apartment's front window until she saw her uncle drive up and park the car. She yelled, "Mama, Uncle Albert is here! I'm going now!" and rushed to get on her winter coat, hat, and scarf and stood at the opened apartment door waiting for her uncle to come up the steps. She yelled down at him, "I'm ready, Uncle Albert. I'm ready!" She quickly hugged her mother, briefly hugged her uncle, and rushed down the stairs and out the door and into the back seat of the car before Albert was out of the apartment carrying the overnight bag she forgot. She would be sleeping at her cousin Julia's house until Sunday.

The cousins were thrilled about being together through the weekend. They used to spend more time in one another's company, but June and her parents moved to a different apartment, a larger one, earlier in 1940. June's father, Henry, got a decent paying job at a manufacturing company in Cicero, Illinois, and they moved from their tiny apartment in Bridgeport to a larger one in Brighton Park. Henry was closer to his new job, and the new apartment had two bedrooms so June could have her own and not be sequestered in a made-over storage space.

Uncle Albert had helped June's father get the job. After all, he thought Henry was a decent guy besides being his wife's brother, and there were some favors that could be called in. Albert only needed to make a couple phone calls. He had connections. Henry's new job was working as a machinist creating molds for lawn sprinklers, but now that it looked like war was on the horizon, the manufacturing company had switched to producing articles for the military. Molds for defense weapons and such. But forty-five cents an hour, and double overtime was not to be ignored. And Henry was grateful to his brother-in-law.

So, the Harris family moved. And June was given her own bedroom. And her mother, Rose, was able to find a part-time job at a local store which helped with the car payment and higher rent, and school clothes and shoes for June. June found some friends at her new school, but Julia was still her *almost sister,* and they were together during many weekends.

The theater was amazing; their seats were perfect; the popcorn was delicious, and the girls loved the movie. There were a few parts which were unexpectedly frightening: the shadows at the start and the graveyard scene at the end, but both June and Julia loved Mickey Mouse as the *Sorcerer's Apprentice.* At the restaurant as they waited for their Chinese dinner, they reviewed the movie, discussed the music, and laughed about Mickey's troubles.

"I think I'd like to command everything just like Mickey did," said Julia, "but I'd know how to control things better than he did. I can always control stuff."

"Well, he was pretty funny doing it. Not so sure you could do it, Julia. It looked hard. But I LOVED the entire movie. I can't wait to go back to school and tell everyone I saw it. Bet no one else did!" and the conversation stopped as the two waiters delivered the chop suey, chow mien, and egg foo young to the table.

The use of the chopsticks was fun but unsuccessful, and the dinner was finished with forks and knives. The girls tried all the strange dishes and liked everything. The advertised "fine tea" was sipped from the delicate rounded cups, and the delicious almond and fortune cookies were enjoyed for dessert. Leftovers were wrapped up to take home.

"OK, girls," said Aunt Maria, "Here's your lunch for tomorrow. Are you ready to go? Do you need to use the washroom before we leave? No? Let's get ready while Dad gets the car for us."

Uncle Albert departed the restaurant carrying the leftovers, and Aunt Maria and the two cousins put their winter coats and hats on and waited just inside the front door of the restaurant. When he pulled up, they hurried to the car and drove back to Julia's house for the weekend.

The girls were tired and didn't stay up late even though it was not just a Friday night but a holiday. Saturday breakfast was pancakes made by the Reynolds' housekeeper, Mrs. Sampson, and lunch was the leftover Chinese food because the housekeeper had Saturday afternoons off if no dinner party was being given. When dinnertime came, Aunt Maria said if they would like a treat, Uncle Albert could go out for White Castle hamburgers and French fries. That was more than acceptable to the girls, and Saturday night dinner was decided.

June and Julia had spent the morning walking around the neighborhood looking at the Christmas decorations and during the remainder of the day, played the new games Julia got for Christmas. There had been no fighting. Yet. It was unusual for them to stay together for such a lengthy time and not have a couple arguments, but June was determined to not spoil her great weekend, and she agreed to do whatever Julia wanted. So far it was a success. That evening, after the hamburgers and French fries, the girls washed up, got their pajamas on, and played additional rounds of Monopoly which, to June's relief, Julia appeared to be winning. Julia insisted on being the banker, and while June thought she saw Julia slip a couple of one-hundred-dollar bills into her growing pile of colorful money, she decided to ignore it. It wasn't worth calling her on her cheating. It wasn't the first time.

"Time to put the game away girls. Then brush your teeth, get into bed. I'll come and tuck you both in." Aunt Maria was also satisfied that no fighting or arguing had occurred.

Games put away, good-nights said, each girl tucked safely into her own twin bed, the darkened bedroom was perfect for a quiet discussion and review of the weekend's activities before falling asleep. Laying in the large, shadowy bedroom, they talked again about the movie reviewing their favorite parts, and giggling about the humor of it. Then June brought up the Chinese dinner and the pancakes and the White Castle hamburgers.

"The food was really great this weekend. I liked the Chinese food, but the hamburgers and the French fries were the best! We never go out to eat. You're lucky, Julia to have parents that do that. I wish we did. Mom says it's healthier to eat the stuff she makes and costs less money too."

Julia's eyes, which were shut, popped open. Money. What had she heard her parents saying about the Harrises and money? Now she remembered, and it was too good not to share.

"Mama said that if my dad hadn't gotten your dad the job he has now, you'd all be walking the streets. Maybe that's why you don't eat out like we do or have a housekeeper to cook and clean like Mrs. Sampson. And your mama has to work at some store. Mine doesn't work because Daddy earns big bucks. Mama says so."

June listened to the comments. She said nothing because she wasn't sure what to say. She didn't know that Uncle Albert got her father a job. She never thought about her mother having to work. Her mother did the housework and cooking and until now, she hadn't considered that the reason her mother worked was to earn additional needed money. She didn't know how to answer Julia and anything she thought of saying might cause a fight, so she closed her eyes and pretended to sleep. She felt Julia turn and look at her, but she remained still until her cousin turned back, rested on her side, and murmured "Good-night."

June lay still for a long time thinking about Julia's words. Finally, she turned on her side too and tried to think about the pleasant parts of the weekend: the movie and the Chinese restaurant and the hamburgers. But the memory of it all had soured, and it took a long time for her to get to sleep. She was kept awake by Julia's words. June hoped her dad would keep his job, that money would not be a problem. She wished her mother didn't need to work and wanted a housekeeper like Mrs. Sampson in their lives. She didn't know what "walking the streets" would be like, but she was sure it would not be agreeable. It sounded miserable.

When she did get to sleep, she dreamed she was the Sorcerer's Apprentice and was having the same trouble as Mickey Mouse had in the movie. The tall pointed hat she wore had dollar signs on it instead of stars, and she was holding perfectly useless French fries instead of a wand. And, despite her desperate attempts, she couldn't control the many hamburgers and chopsticks which were dancing around her, mocking her, laughing loudly, and pointing to the open door which led outside to a long, dark, dangerous street.

Chapter 5   #1 Mrs. Sampson

When I was first interviewed by Mrs. Reynolds for the job of housekeeper (and cook and nanny, as it turned out), she thought it important to hear my entire story. She could easily check my work background, and I wasn't worried about that. I was an excellent worker, never a day sick or late, and always polite and accurate with the keeping to my tasks. She wanted to know about me personally, so I told her. I was the oldest of six siblings, so having helped to care for and raise my brothers and sisters, I knew about children. I finished grade seven, but could not go on with my education because I was needed at home. My father had died by the time I was thirteen, and I began to work part-time as an assistant housekeeper so learned my trade. I married and widowed at a young age. My late and much missed husband, David Sampson, had been killed in a terrible accident down in southern Illinois where we lived. It was difficult to make a living there, so three of my older sisters and I moved to Chicago where they all married and were currently spread about the city with their families. I had a small room in a boarding house close by, and on my next birthday I would be twenty-eight years old.

It was all a lie, but she accepted it, and through the years, I have kept to the story. In truth, I have one younger sister, Theresa, and we live together in a small basement apartment where Ma died. Don't remember my father. I'm unsure Ma was married though she claimed to be. My sister is a decent seamstress and works from our apartment while I invented a name for myself and got hired as a housekeeper. I never married, but in my experience, unmarried women were often turned away from important jobs, so I became a widow and renamed myself *Eliza Sampson*, remembering the name *Sampson* from a story of someone who was strong. I barely finished sixth grade and was glad to be done with that education nonsense, and while I was younger than Mrs. Reynolds, I made myself to be older by about five years. I once considered being an actress.

I was hired because Maria Reynolds accepted my story and sincerity, and because she was overburdened with young Julia and the care of a large house and the dinner parties she was expected to host. She hired me on the spot because when Julia began to cry, there was such a look of dismay on her face that I felt sorry for her and said, "Ma'am, allow me to get the child and show what I can do." She pointed the way to the nursery, and I went to Julia. She had gotten herself all wrapped up in a blanket, was wet and hungry, so once I took care of her needs, she was fine, and I was hired as: *Mrs. Sampson, Housekeeper.*

When you care for a child daily as I ended up doing, there is a connection created, no matter the actual relationship. That is what happened with Julia who was not an easy child. She was babied by her father, and while she had a decent relationship with her mother, I saw a strain between them as she grew. Maria and Albert Reynolds had only one child, and all the toys in the world couldn't make up for Julia's loneliness. She had few friends and spent time with her cousin, June, another child I became attached to and fond of. I watched and listened to the two of them as they played and noted that Julia was not kind. She could be ornery and quarrelsome if she didn't get her way, and I noticed many times when Julia was plain old mean to her cousin.

The Reynolds were fair to me, but I earned it. I never figured out what Albert Reynolds did as work although I had some ideas. Through the difficulties of the Depression, none of the family wanted. There was plenty. If dairy or meat was in short supply in the city, no one would know it in the Reynolds' house. If I needed something for a dinner or we were running low on pantry supplies, I would just let Mrs. Reynolds know. She would write it on a piece of paper and put it on Mr. Reynolds' desk. The supplies would appear in a day or so. Sometimes faster. I never questioned where they came from, and I never asked about the various men coming in and out of the house or the big boxes which were delivered early in the mornings or late at night and taken down to the basement area, a place I was told to stay away from. I did. I didn't want to show any curiosity about those things. I never questioned the wine and spirits which seemed to be available despite the law against them. I learned early to do my job and shut my mouth.

I did earn a decent wage, and when I needed additional kitchen help for a large dinner party or the twice-yearly heavy cleaning which was done, I was given leave to hire helpers. That is how my sister came to work with me at times. I told her to make herself a few maid uniforms and taught her how to serve and set tables, how to pour and stand, and when a party required more than just my assistance, she was hired. She did her job and worked, and I never saw any reason to let Mrs. Reynolds know that it was my sister who was discharging her fancy wine into those showy stemmed glasses. Even when Theresa married, she still was able to earn extra by helping me. It all worked out.

I even had a "Housekeeper Quarters" which was available for my use. Most nights I went home, but sometimes, especially on the late-night dinner parties or the weekend trips the Mr. and Mrs. liked to take, I stayed there. The room was not just used by me. When her parents went on trips, Julia wanted to sleep with me, and I allowed it. She was in her large bedroom and said she was afraid, and I understood. It was one thing when there was a noisy party or she heard her parents' talking downstairs because the sounds of others comforted her. But when the two of us were alone in the house, well, even I was glad for the little girl's company. She would sit at the kitchen table drawing and talking to me as I made dinner for us or cleaned up. We occasionally baked cookies, and I would let her decorate them with the brown-sugar icing she liked. Times like these were cozy. We were like a mother and daughter although Julia never called me anything but Mrs. Sampson.

One Saturday night, when her parents were out of town, we were in the kitchen, and she was drawing and coloring hearts on sheets of paper. It was near Valentine's Day, and she was working on a special drawing for her father. She was coloring and chatting away, and I was finishing up the pots and pans. I had some of the silver out to polish. I knew next weekend there would be a dinner party, and I was trying to get a head start on my work.

"Mrs. Sampson, don't you have any children?" and she kept coloring in the large heart she had drawn.

"No, Julia," I answered as I bent down to wipe the floor where I spilled some water, "I wasn't married long, and my husband died, and we never had any." I thought it best to stick with my original story. It had been a few years, and frankly, I was starting to believe it.

"Well, I decided that when I get married, I am going to have children. Me and my husband are going to have two. Do you want to know about them?"

"Of course; tell me."

"My husband and me are going to have two children, and they are both going to be girls. And they are going to be the same age. What's that called again?"

"Do you mean they are going to be *twins*?"

"That's right. They are going to be twins. And then they are going to be best friends."

"I hope things turn out that way for you."

"Oh, they will. My children are going to be best friends and talk and play together and have fun. Because there are two of them, they will have someone to play games with. They won't have to wait until their girl cousin comes over to play games with her. And my husband and me will play the games too."

I didn't have the heart to tell her that you needed a brother or sister to have cousins for your children. Perhaps her husband would have some. I just said, "That sounds like fun."

"It will be fun. And they will both sleep in their own bed in the same room. Just like the two beds I have in my room, but there is no one in the other bed. And they won't be lonely at night. Or scared. Because they will have each other. And their parents, that's my husband and me, will always be with them and make sure they are happy. Isn't that a great idea?" and she held up her paper, put it to the side, and began to draw another heart.

I had completed the pots and pans. I sat down at the table across from her, picked up the first piece of silver and began to rub. "That does sound like a good idea, Julia. I hope it all turns out for you. Twins would be wonderful."

"And you can come and live at my house and help me with them. Will you do that? "

I looked at her and smiled. "Well, we'll see. That's way in the future."

Julia nodded her head. "Yes, it is, but it *will* be like that. And I will have my Daddy make sure it does work out like that. He said he'd do anything for me. That's why I want to make a BIG heart for him."

I had to ask, "And one for your Mama too?"

Julia turned her head to the side and thought. "I guess so, but hers won't be so big," and she drew and colored.

I polished the silver, and she chattered on about the hearts and her twins and her future. And I hoped, I sincerely hoped, it would be a happy one.

Chapter 6   Doubting

She began to doubt her sanity. Why would she even consider the act of murder? Yes, Julia was annoying. She always had been. All their lives. June decided she should put up and shut up. She had made many friends in this lovely neighborhood, kept active in various clubs, and attended many events opened to the residents. She appreciated all the money Julia uses for their living arrangement, and where else would she live? Her house, the one she and Peter bought and lived in, the one in which they had raised their two children, was gone. Sold. She had been fair and given a large portion of that money to Julia to help with the townhouse because that was merited. There was no place she could rent with the money she received monthly. At least, nothing as nice as this. June did not want to bother her children who had lives of their own and had no room for her anyway. She doubted they even wanted her.

After the smelly dog poop incident, she had washed the floor and then, to made sure there was no remaining smell, sprayed some air freshener even though she hated the smell. Julia liked it. Julia bought it. Julia used it. Then June went to the deck and washed off both her shoes and set them at the corner to dry in the late evening sun. However, the next morning they were still wet and mostly ruined. She could probably wear them for her walks, but now she would need to look for some shoe sales. She needed new shoes anyway. She doubted this pair would have lasted much longer.

After her cleaning, she went into her bedroom and ran a hot bath. She poured Epsom salts into the tub and placed a few drops of lavender oil into the water before sinking into the warmth. When she toweled off and brushed through her mostly gray hair (Julia thought she needed to dye it and kept telling her she would look better with youthful brown hair. June refused.) and put her nightgown on, she looked around for her *Bible*. She knew there were passages speaking out against murder. She needed to read those, to clear her mind, to settle her soul. But she couldn't find the book. After fifteen minutes, she settled on her bed with the new edition of one of the many magazines to which Julia subscribed. She would look for the *Bible* in the morning.

The following days passed wordlessly. In the morning, Julia stayed in her bedroom until June left for one of her classes. Lunchtime was ignored. Dinner was eaten separately: June in the kitchen and Julia in the front room watching television. The cousins had known each other for more than seven decades, and they had weathered their share of fights through the years, and soon, June was sure, one of them would give in and speak to the other ending the chilliness. She doubted it would be Julia.

It wasn't. A few days later as she was making breakfast, Julia came to the kitchen and sat at the table. June turned and said, "Good morning. Making eggs this morning. Do you want scrambled or hard boiled?" With those words, the silence was ended, a truce engendered.

That is not to say things were perfect. They weren't. Julia had a delicate sense of smell, so she claimed, and once or twice, as June returned from her walk, Julia's delicate, slightly upturned nose (She had rhinoplasty when she was fifty. A gift to herself.) lifted and checked the air, and she cocked her head to one side, waiting to say something. But June took no chances and remembered to remove her ragged shoes, leaving them at the edge of the deck. For a time, she avoided the wooded walking path, and when she did resume walking there, was observantly careful where she stepped. June doubted any unpleasant smell would follow her in again.

Peace restored, the cousins eased back into their customary relationship. At times Julia would mention a touchy subject which could have led to another disagreement, but June was careful in her answer and made every attempt to mollify her cousin. Twice, Julia was asked to accompany June on her evening walks, and she agreed. On those nights, they did not walk the path around the lake but kept to the winding streets in the complex. As they went down one side of the street and up the other, Julia could easily track her neighbors' doings. She could see who was redecorating, who was sitting outside, who was entertaining company, who was fighting loudly enough to be heard. She would make comments to June about her observations, seemingly content to walk and wander and whisper.

Those evening walks were short, but June was glad for them. It seemed such a normal and ordinary thing to do: to stroll with Julia. As they meandered, she began to replace the doubt about her sanity, the doubt about her terrible thoughts, the doubt about the relationship she had with her cousin with a delicate amount, a fragile bit, a Lilliputian quantity of hope.

Chapter 7   1945 Age 15

When they were fifteen and in their sophomore year of high school, Julia stole June's boyfriend, Kenneth. To be fair, he was not really her boyfriend. They hadn't dated and only talked during the one high school class they had together. But June liked Kenneth and thought he liked her and decided to ask him to the Sadie Hawkins Dance the school was planning to hold in late November. She mentioned this to Julia who also had one class with Kenneth, just so Julia would observe his looks and manner. Although Julia didn't know who he was, she paid attention in that class, and before June even got a chance, or the nerve, to bring the dance up to Kenneth, Julia stopped him after class one day and asked him to go. Kenneth agreed. It was so unfair.

But so was the fact that Julia and June were at the same high school. They were slated to attend different schools because they were in different school boundaries. When June's family moved into the larger apartment, away from Julia's family, the girls, who had gone to the same elementary school, were separated during grades six, seven, and eight. They attended different schools, had different experiences, met different people, and made different friends. During the quiet times in her own bedroom, thinking about the change, June admitted to herself that it was a good one. For her. She had always dwelt in the shadow of her cousin who was better dressed, better coifed, better organized, just better than she was. At least June felt this way. She felt this way because Julia claimed these things.

"June, isn't my new jacket cute? Too bad yours is so old. Is your mother going to fix that torn pocket?"

"June, look at my new shoes. Aren't they darling? Too bad you don't have some like it, but I guess your old ones are fine."

"June, do you like the way Mama fixed my hair today? These bows are brand-new and Mama bought them at Marshall Field's yesterday. They were expensive. She said so."

"June, look at my new notebooks and school rucksack Mama got me. Isn't it great? Look, I can put things in the zippered sides. I'm the first person to have one in our class. I'll get a new one next year, and I'll give you this old one then."

June looked at everything and nodded and told Julia it was all great, and she was lucky to have it, and yes, she wished she could have them too. Thoughts about money swirled around her brain creating a slight headache. Then she swallowed her jealousy and marched to the classroom in her old shoes, wearing her torn jacket, clutching her books in her arms, and feeling her unbowed pigtails bounce on the sides of her head. And then her cousin wound up in the same high school.

She was not supposed to go to Hamilton High with June. In Julia's school district, all high school students went to Greenburg Technical High School, but she did not want to go there. For one thing, it was a *Technical School*, whatever that meant, and Julia had no intention of attending the same school as all those spiteful, loathsome girls who lived close to her and had bullied her for years. She knew she was better than they were. Hamilton High was not that far away, and it was newer, and many of the students who attended there also went to college since it was a *College Prep* school. Julia cried to her father that she needed to be prepared for college and didn't he want her to earn a college degree? So, Uncle Albert made some phone calls. He had connections. He was able to make certain special arrangements for his daughter. People always owed him a favor or two, and Julia received privileged permission to attend Hamilton High School, the same school her cousin June would attend.

During their freshman year, June was grateful for the company. She and Julia had most of their classes together, and that made it easier to maneuver through the hallways and the sea of girls who were there. Because so many of the male students, once they reached their eighteenth year, joined a branch of the military to assist in the war effort, there was a large female population. That made younger male students, like Kenneth, prime dating material, and June was determined to ask him to the dance. But she who hesitates…and Julia got there first.

When Julia told June that she had asked Kenneth to the Sadie Hawkins Dance and he agreed to go, June was flabbergasted. They were at the bus stop waiting for the next bus home, and June thought she had misheard. Certainly, she had misheard.

"Wait, are you talking about Kenneth Abernathy, the boy I was going to ask to the dance? THAT Kenneth? The one in MY English class? Julia, you knew I was going to ask him!"

Julia waved at someone across the street before answering. "I guess that's the same one who is in MY algebra class. You didn't ask him. You only mentioned it, and it was such a long time ago, I didn't think you were serious."

"Long time ago? I just told you last week and I just hadn't gotten around to it. I was going to do it this week! I can't believe you would do this! This is beyond mean, Julia; it's underhanded, and you know that!"

Julia shrugged as she got in line for the bus which had just pulled up, and replied in a nonchalant way, "It's just a dance, June. You can always go with some of the other girls, or maybe one of the freshman boys needs a date. Or that *Patriotic Girls Group* is always looking for help. You can still go to the dance," and Julia climbed on the bus while June backed up and out of line. She waited for the next bus and sat in a back seat by herself, considering what action to take, determining her future conduct, deciding what to do.

Nothing. That's what she could do. Nothing. She wanted to go to the dance, but wouldn't go with a bunch of girls, and there were no freshman boys she even knew. And she liked Kenneth. She was angry and hurt and disheartened by her cousin's devious action. Reflecting on the incident, she realized the one thing she wasn't was truly surprised. This was typical of Julia. She did things like this. Julia was selfish and could be mean. She could also be kind and giving, but those instances were rare. June couldn't be around her; she was determined to ignore her. At least for a time. She would get an earlier morning bus and a later afternoon one so she didn't have to ride with her. She would go to the school library during her lunch period so she didn't need to sit next with her in the lunchroom. She would sign up with the *Patriotic Girls Group* at school and help them in the war effort by selling cupcakes at the dance where all proceeds were to go to the bonds and stamps sales which would support their fighting men. She would not sit at home the night of the dance feeling sorry for herself. Not this time.

At the *Patriotic Girls Group* planning meeting, the group decided to wear navy skirts, white blouses, and a red kerchief so they would look like a team, a patriotic team. June was glad this was the uniform because she had all the parts. Had she asked Kenneth to the dance, she would have wanted to ask her parents for a new dress, and she was sure there wasn't money for one. *This is better in the long run*, she thought. *I'm helping the country and the group and doing my part. That's more than I can say for Julia. The sneak.*

On the night of the dance, her father drove her and dropped her off near the school's gymnasium an hour before the dance would start. The *Patriotic Girls Group* had decided that they needed that hour to set up the cupcakes, punch, and napkins. June straightened her skirt, retied her red kerchief, and found the group. She smiled and greeted the other girls, took a tray of cupcakes, and placed them on the table.

June managed to stay in the background. Even when the Assistant Principal thanked the *Patriotic Girls Group* for their volunteer service and asked them to come out for the applause they so deserved, June concealed herself in the back, shrinking down so she would not be noticed. But Julia saw her and waved and blew her kisses, and when the music began again, she came over to the table where the treats were being sold and sought out June who was cleaning up a dropped cupcake. Julia stood close to her until June noticed.

"Hey, June," she said, "I'm glad that you're here tonight. I think what this group is doing is wonderful, and I wanted to tell you that I miss sitting on the bus with you and eating lunch with you. I hope you won't be mad at me anymore. After all, we're related. Aren't we *almost sisters?*"

June finished wiping the frosting up and stood. She looked at her cousin and sighed. Julia had made the first move, and, really, they were close. Almost sisters. "I guess," she answered. "Actually, I've missed you too," and June sighed again.

"Good," smiled Julia. "And just so you know, you aren't missing much with Kenneth. He's a bad dancer and doesn't want to dance anyway. He just wants to talk about boring sports, and if you want to date him, I'm sure he'll go out with you. In fact, I can say something if you want me to."

"NO!' and June shook her head. "Don't, Julia. It doesn't matter now anyway. I'll be on the regular bus on Monday morning. Save me a seat?"

"You bet!" and Julia grinned. "Well, have to get back to Kooky Kenny. See you Monday morning," and Julia left to find her date.

June watched her go. She couldn't see in the crowd exactly where her cousin went, and didn't see Kenneth, but now it didn't matter. She no longer cared. She didn't want to date him anymore. Not now. She thought, *I don't need another worn-out rucksack from Julia. She is the way she is*. June threw the smashed cupcake and napkin into the garbage and told the girl in change she was going to the bathroom to wash the frosting from her hands.

Chapter 8   Hoping

June finished her morning ablutions, walked into the kitchen to make their breakfast, and was startled to see a large gift bag on the kitchen table with a piece of paper hanging from the side which proclaimed "For June". It was not June's birthday. It was not Christmas or any holiday, but she had received a gift from Julia. This was surprising and an immediate hopeful feeling arose in June. Perhaps Julia was changing. Could change. Would change. The last couple weeks since the dog poop incident had been difficult. The cousins did not speak for a time, and then, gradually, grudgingly, resumed their relationship. Perhaps this was a form of apology from Julia. June hoped it was. For some reason she thought of a poem from high school. Something about hope being "a thing with feathers", and she felt happy.

She thought maybe she should wait until Julia came to the kitchen to open it but was so anxious to find out what it was, she decided to unwrap the gift. She removed the tissue paper and lifted out an awkwardly large box which declared that it contained a new and expensive (June knew this because she had priced the item and decided she could not afford to purchase the luxury.) coffee maker. That new kind. The kind that made one cup of coffee at a time and used individually wrapped and marvelously created small capsules which held the exact amount of coffee needed for one perfect and delicious cup.

June let out a small gasp of surprise and delight. Then she wondered: Why? Setting aside the question, she reached into the gift bag where three small differently-colored boxes were quartered, took them out, and placed them on the table to examine. She just knew what they were. She absolutely expected them to be those small individual capsules containing the perfect amount of measured coffee grounds for the ultimately delicious cup of steaming coffee. She removed her glasses which were hanging from her neckline, wiped them off with the edge of her blouse, and placed them on her face. She sat down to examine the types of coffee offered and thought she would read the description on the boxes and spend time considering which one she would have this morning after she read the directions for the use of the machine.

June looked at the boxes, noting that each contained a dozen small capsules and read the labels: *Pure Peppermint Tea, Chamomile Tea, English Breakfast Tea.* She sat back in the chair and looked at the boxes once more, this time picking them up and turning them over just to verify that they contained tea and not coffee. Then she stood up to investigate the gift bag just in case she missed additional boxes. It was empty. June looked behind the colorful bag and over to the counter and under the table, but there was nothing else. Julia had given her TEA.

She sat back down realizing she knew the answer to "Why?" She and her cousin had often discussed their preferences for drinks, and June was certain Julia knew she did not like tea. If she felt ill, she would have some peppermint tea, but that was it. It was medicinal. The coffee maker obviously brewed tea. Here were the capsules to verify that. However, June did not want any. If she did want tea, couldn't she drink the same tea as Julia? Wasn't she allowed to drink the imported Harrington Tea? Immediately, June perceived the truth: she was not. That tea was too expensive, too exclusive to share. She wasn't special enough to share in the imported tea. This was her cousin's attempt to stop her from drinking coffee simply because Julia did not like the smell of it. She was trying to change her, attempting to remake her, to mold her, to shape, transform, recondition her, and June would not have it. This was just one of a long series of attempts made by Julia throughout the years. Attempts to amend what Julia perceived as June's faults. A snippet of anger wound itself through the back of June's spine and up to her head where a small headache began. She tried taking some deep, cleansing breaths so the anger would disappear.

There was some sound. A bedroom door opened, and Julia came into the kitchen. She saw that June had opened her gift and smiled.

"So, what do you think? I had the store deliver it a couple days ago when you were exercising, and thought you would like this surprise. Do you?"

June expelled one of the cleansing breaths, and spoke. "Julia, thank you for the gift. I know you took the effort to get it, and I don't want you to think I don't appreciate it. I have admired these new coffee makers and you know I can't afford one, so it's a generous gift. But you gave me boxes of tea. I don't drink tea. You know that. Perhaps when I go to the store, I can pick up some of the capsules and try the coffee. That would be great," and June began to clean up the tissue and moved the coffee maker to the end of the counter. She took the three boxes of tea and placed them into the cabinet next to the imported Harrington tea tin. Then she took the glass coffee carafe from her decades old coffee maker, filled it with water, and started her morning coffee.

Julia sat at the table, an incredulous look on her face, and watched her. "Do you mean to say you aren't even going to try the tea?

That disgusting coffee smell fills the kitchen and keeps me from enjoying my own drink. I told you that tea is healthier than coffee, and I've been telling you that for years. You should listen to me. Just look at the difference in our sizes, and I have been a tea drinker forever! Putting all that cream in your coffee just forms mucus and adds weight. I thought I was doing you a favor, but I guess not," and Julia crossed her arms over her chest.

June didn't answer her. This had been an ongoing argument since they moved in together, and she was tired of it. She didn't understand why Julia hated the smell of coffee in this house, but never complained all the years her husband drank it. Or at all the restaurants they visited. Or at other people's houses. Just here. Just June's coffee.

Once her coffee was started, she began to organize Julia's tea. As she put the water on to boil and got the Harrington tea tin down, Julia stood up.

"Fine, June, I'm not going to argue with you about this matter. I was just trying to do something nice for you and help you to stay heathy. I'm going to watch my morning shows in the front room so I don't have to smell the coffee. Take that tray, and bring the tea to me there. All I want for breakfast is some toast. You know the way I like it," and Julia turned and went into the front room and turned on the television.

June took the tray from the top of the refrigerator and the toaster from the bottom cabinet. She got the butter out and opened a new jar of the imported Sicilian orange marmalade Julia ate. The only kind she ate. "We had this when we were in Sicily," she once told June, "It's very expensive, but it's the only kind I like." Personally, June liked the grape jelly that was ninety-nine cents when on sale at the grocery store. *But,* she thought, *to each her own.*

June prepared the tea tray for her cousin, placed a napkin alongside the plate which held the toast, and brought it in to the front room. At least Julia had the courtesy to thank her.

"Thanks. Put it there on the coffee table," and Julia didn't look at June or realize the irony of her instructions.

June returned to the kitchen where her coffee was waiting for her. She poured herself a cup, opened the refrigerator and removed the carton of creamer, readying her own morning drink. She sat at the table thinking she was not hungry and would skip breakfast. Instead, after her coffee, she would take a morning walk. Maybe she would go to her friend Alice's house and ask if she wanted to walk with her. The late summer day was warm but not humid or sticky. The sun was out and a light breeze was noticeable. She thought time in the fresh air would bring back her appetite and help her damaged mood. The day had started out as hopeful.

June sipped her coffee and looked at the box containing the new coffee maker. Later she would take a trip to the store and price the coffee capsules. It was a shame to let the maker go to waste, and perhaps if just one cup at a time were made, the smell would not be overpowering for Julia. She sipped again at her morning drink, listened to Julia talk back to the television, and felt the hope that had greeted her when she saw the gift box drift down to the floor, a small white downy feather turning to dust.

"Hope" is the thing with feathers

Emily Dickinson

"Hope" is the thing with feathers –

That perches in the soul –

And sings the tune without the words –

And never stops – at all –

And sweetest – in the Gale – is heard –

And sore must be the storm –

That could abash the little Bird

That kept so many warm –

I've heard it in the chillest land –

And on the strangest Sea –

Yet – never – in Extremity,

It asked a crumb – of me.

Chapter 9   1950 Age 20

June searched her pocket for a clean handkerchief and not finding one, she got a box of tissues and put it in front of Julia who immediately grabbed a handful and blew her nose. She sat down next to her cousin at the kitchen table and waited for her to stop weeping. It was a warm night in the middle of July. June arrived home from her classes only to discover Julia waiting for her on the front porch. She was seated on the top step and was crying. June didn't know what happened, but since Julia rarely cried, she knew it was serious.

"Julia, are you OK? Are Aunt Maria and Uncle Albert OK? What wrong? Come on in and sit down," and June opened the front door and led her cousin to the kitchen where she turned on the light, switched the table fan to *low*, and searched for a handkerchief.

Julia blew her nose again saying, "I need some water, and maybe you can make me some tea." June got a glass of water for her and began to heat some for the tea. Julia took a few sips and sighed. "I was hoping someone would be home here. My parents are fine. They are out to a dinner party, and I forgot yours went away for the weekend. I just heard some awful news and needed to share it. Jonathan Belcher is dead. He was killed in a battle in Korea, and I just found out. It happened last week, and his sister, Patricia, called me today. I was so upset I came here to talk to you or maybe Aunt Rose," and she blew her nose again.

"Oh no, how horrible!" and June sat down again. She patted Julia's arm and set the cup of hot water and a teabag before her. She poured herself a glass of water and sat at the table, waiting for Julia to create her tea, blow her nose, and compose herself.

Jonathan Belcher had been Julia's boyfriend during much of the last two years of high school. When they graduated and Julia went away to college, Jonathan joined the army, and they decided they would end their relationship. But of course, they would remain friends. When discussing the breakup with her cousin, Julia explained that the small college she was going to (Uncle Albert made a couple phone calls because Julia's grades weren't exactly spectacular. He had connections.) was said to be a great place to meet a smart and handsome man ("Going to work on my MRS. degree!" Julia laughed.) and while Julia and Jonathan never spoke or saw each other again, she liked to explain they parted friends.

Julia lasted for one year at college. She had a great time. Her grades demonstrated it. "The classes were really boring," she told June. "There was so much reading they expected you to do. It was unreasonable! And the papers and research! Well, I'm better off here at home. I'm going to take some time off to relax and maybe find a job after this summer. I just need to rest for a few months." She did rest. She rested through the summer of 1949, and in the fall, because she complained of boredom, her father gave her a part-time job in his office.

"It's just some filing and telephone answering and a bit of typing I have to do," she explained to June. "Of course, I can't type well. Not like you. Probably should have paid attention in that stupid high school class we had to take. But I only need to work about twenty hours a week, so that's good," and she showed June the suits and blouses and shoes she had bought to look *professional but still chic*, as she explained.

June admired her new clothing and listened to Julia talk about how college was just not for her and silently wished college had been offered to her, but there was no money (and no assisting telephone calls) for it, although her grades had been excellent. She worked for the year after high school to save money so she could take some classes at a downtown business school. On the night Julia came over to tell her about Jonathan, she had just come home from her Friday class and was looking forward to getting to bed early. She had to work tomorrow. She worked part-time job at Montgomery Ward Department Store in the Children's Department, and every Saturday morning she was expected to arrive at the store early. She could not send Julia away when she was so upset, so she continued to sit and commiserate with her.

Once Julia calmed down, she looked around the kitchen. "Is there anything to eat? I didn't eat dinner and am hungry, and Mrs. Sampson wasn't home. She had today off for some reason. Didn't Aunt Rose leave you some dinner?"

"No," replied June. "I told her I could figure out dinner for myself while they are gone. I was just going to scramble some eggs and have them with toast."

"Sound good. I'll have the same. Going to go to the bathroom to splash water on my face. Be back in a sec," and Julia rose from the table, leaving a stack of soggy tissues.

June signed and clean up the mess. She washed her hands at the sink, got out a pan and the toaster, broke the eggs into a bowl and beat them while adding salt and pepper. She measured butter into the pan, got out the bread and jam, and kept busy while she heard the water running in the bathroom. The table was set, eggs were almost ready, and the toast was just popping up as Julia came out and sat down at the table. June had filled the coffee maker with coffee and water, and asked Julia if she wanted some.

"Oh no; no vile coffee. I hate the smell. I'll just have more tea. Do you have some peppermint tea? That would be much better for my stomach which is a bit upset. After all, I've had a real shock," and June opened the cabinet pulling out the peppermint tea, refilled the tea kettle, and set it back on the stove.

Dinner was ready and served. She filled up a cup with hot water for Julia's tea, ignored the coffee maker, and poured herself additional iced water. She sat at the table across from Julia, and they began to eat.

"You know," said Julia chewing her toast, "for a time, I thought Jonathan and I would get married after high school. But then he began to talk about joining the army and asked me what I thought. I had to be honest and told him that he could do what he wanted, but if he did that, I didn't see a future for us. I saw myself married to a college graduate who had a white-collar job and made good money. After all, I am used to nicer things and don't plan to work after marriage. I'm going to raise a family. Two children, most likely. I think I hurt his feelings, but then, after graduation and my plans to go to college, he saw I was serious. The way things turned out, it really was for the best. Jonathan was a nice boy, and we had fun, but really, I could never see myself married to him. These eggs taste good. Is there any more toast? I didn't realize how hungry I was," and she looked around at the toaster and then at June.

June got up and put additional pieces of bread into the toaster. "Do you want more eggs? They won't take long to make."

"Well, as long as you are up, sure," and Julia put the last bit of egg on her last bite of toast and waited to be served. "I am tired, and this has been an upsetting time. A meal makes me feel better."

June continued making additional food for her cousin. "Did you work late tonight?"

"No, I didn't work today at all. I told Daddy I couldn't work on Fridays. That's my usual shopping day. Sometimes Mama and I shop together because we like to get the best buys before the Saturday shoppers. I got the cutest skirt and top today. I'll wear it when I work next week. June, do you know that if I had married Jonathan and gotten this news, that would make me a *widow*! What an awful thought. A widow at age twenty! Well, I suppose things turned out for the best. Oh, thanks. The eggs look great," and Julia began to butter her freshly delivered toast.

June sat down to finish her last few cold bites. She chewed and swallowed and then asked, "Are you going to go over and see Jonathan's parents? Or at least call them? After all, you did go together almost two years, and Patricia did call you. I always liked her. We had several high school classes together."

Julia swallowed. She sat back in her chair and sighed before speaking. "I don't think so. If there is a service of some sort, I guess I'll have to go, but I don't think I need to telephone. Instead, I'll have Mama and Daddy send a big fancy flower arrangement to their house and I'll write a nice note with it. Something like: *Sorry about Jonathan*, or maybe *I'm remembering the great times your son and I had*, or…I don't know. I'll think of something. Maybe we should just sign it *From the Reynolds Family*. I'll ask Mama tomorrow. Anyway, I feel better. Do you want to play some cards or a game of some kind? I can stay the night if you want me to. Aren't you afraid to be in this house by yourself?"

June began to clear the table, putting dishes in the sink and replacing the foods. "No, I'm not afraid. You're welcome to stay, but I don't feel up to playing any games. I have an early morning tomorrow and need to get to work. But if you need to stay and talk some more, we can."

Julia sighed again. "No, I guess I'll get home. Mama and Daddy should be there by now. I should tell them the sad news in person. Thanks anyway, June. Will we see you for Sunday dinner?"

June nodded, and she continued to clean up.

"Great. Alright, I'm going to go now. Lock up after me and see you in a couple of days. Can't wait to show you the new outfit! Think I'll wear it and make an impression on that new guy Dad just hired. His name is Arnold, and I'm sure he's a college grad. He's really cute! Good-night," and she got the keys to her car out. The car Uncle Albert bought her because she told him that taking public transportation to his office was getting her new *professional but still chic* clothes dirty, and didn't he want her to look good as she worked in his office?

June walked Julia out and watched as she drove away. She returned to the kitchen, completed the cleaning, and turned off the kitchen lights. She walked into the front room and looked at her books and notes from her classes, but decided that she would review the material tomorrow night after work. She picked up the telephone book placed next to the telephone to look up a number which she then dialed. When the voice on the other end said *Hello*, June replied, "Hello, Patricia. This is June Harris. Do you have a minute to talk? Yes, that's why I'm calling," and she sat down and spoke kind and heartfelt words and listened to Patricia's sobs.

Chapter 10   #2 Mrs. Sampson

When my sister, Theresa, got married and asked if she and her husband could have the basement apartment as theirs, I agreed. Then I went to Mrs. Reynolds and told another lie. I said that my apartment building was being sold and all the tenants were asked to move or pay twice as much rent, and was it possible for me to live in the Housekeeper's Quarters? She told me I could, and I spent the next two days moving the rest of my clothes and the few personal items I had into the rooms. Neither Mr. or Mrs. Reynolds spoke to me about paying rent, and I never mentioned it either. Since I continued to receive the same salary and was never charged any rent, I was able to save some money for my future. I was a diligent and consistent worker, never stole anything of great value from them, and kept whatever secrets I learned about them, so I figure it was a fair trade.

I lived rent-free in the Reynolds house, and because I was there most of the time, there was a gradual shifting of responsibilities concerning Julia from her mother to me. Mr. Reynolds was constantly busy with his work and office and meetings, and Mrs. Reynolds became quite the social leader in several women's clubs. I prepared a luncheon for one of her club meetings at least once a month. I don't remember all the names, and she often changed clubs, but the one I silently snickered at was the "Chicago Society Women's Literary and Reading Discussion Group". The dozen or so women who showed up read mostly the newspaper gossip columns, and discussions were usually about the women who didn't show up. They enjoyed the cheese souffle I was usually asked to serve, and they ate many of the small homemade dessert creampuffs, but what they managed to really appreciate were the Bee's Knees cocktails I made for them. I was kept busy mixing the gin, honey, and lime juice, and could hardly keep up with the demand. Luckily, they had drivers to take them home. As large as the Reynolds' house was, I'm unsure there were enough bedrooms to let all the ladies sleep it off.

I suppose these clubs did some good. I know they had various dinners and dances and drives where the proceeds, at least part of them, went to help some charities. Mrs. Reynolds was proud of her work and kept a book with newspaper clippings containing her name and her pictures. Between the dinner parties with friends and business associates, the club meetings and activities, and her weekly Friday shopping trips, Mrs. Reynolds barely had time to spend with her daughter, Julia. So, I did.

Julia seemed to be a happy child for the first ten years of her life, but something happened after that. I believe it was partly due to the Harris family's move to another neighborhood. Her cousin June was her best friend. Practically her only friend, and I know she missed seeing her in school and spending weekends with her. Problems started in sixth grade, and Julia sometimes came home and cried at the kitchen table as I tried to comfort her. I didn't get much out of her except that some of the older girls in the neighborhood were "picking" on her and calling her names. *Rich Brat* was one of the names they called her, but she had a fit when I said her parents should know about the problem.

"NO! Don't mention it to them. Those girls will find out, and it will only become worse," she blubbered as she wiped her nose on her sleeve.

Perhaps I should have said something, but I know girls, especially at that age, can be troublesome, and I didn't want a bad situation to get worse. I felt sorry for the girl and in part, wasn't completely sure this was my charge, so I kept quiet. I watched Julia and tried to be there for her to talk to because Mrs. Reynolds was usually not home. The situation did improve. Eventually Julia stopped her crying and complaining. She didn't always seem happy, but she settled down. She was kept busy with the activities her mother arranged for her, but she never gained many friends in the neighborhood.

From the age of five, Julia had after school activities to attend. She started dancing lessons at a young age and continued until she outright refused to go to them. There were piano lessons and singing lessons and art lessons. It became my responsibility to gather her and her sheet music or ballet slippers or art supplies and have Roy, the Reynolds' driver, transport us to the house or academy or studio. Sometimes I waited in a small sitting room, and other times I went out to the automobile to stay. Over the years, Roy and I became friendly, and I learned about his wife and five children, and as our friendship progressed, he confided to me some of the secrets involving Mr. Reynolds. Secrets I kept. I know the importance of a closed mouth.

Julia was not talented. Part of being a decent dancer, singer, musician, or artist involves the actual practice of the art. That much I did know. Julia did not practice. She made a swipe at everything. When Mrs. Reynolds remembered to ask Julia about her lessons and her practicing, Julia answered that things were going well, and yes, she had practiced. Or was planning to after dinner. Or before school. Or on the weekend. That seemed to be enough for her parents. Her teachers always assured the Reynolds that Julia was *coming along nicely* and *showing progress* and *making headway*. The Depression years had left marks on everyone. Fewer students equaled less money. Unfounded encouragement was crucial.

Julia did the same thing with her schoolwork. I tried to help her, but my sixth-grade education only went so far. She got by. And her parents seemed fine with the average grades she made. If she passed her subjects and didn't get into trouble, they seemed to be satisfied. Mr. and Mrs. Reynolds always met the teachers, gave them gifts for Christmas, and showed up when parents were expected to. I guess they were making a swipe too.

By the end of eighth grade, Julia was teeming with willfulness and stubbornness, and often argued with her mother. She refused additional dancing or music lessons, but continued art lessons for a time before she quit those. There was an elite, expensive high school which was downtown and which Mrs. Reynolds wanted her to attend. She refused. Julia went to her father to complain, and he made arrangements for her to attend the same high school as her cousin, June. Mrs. Reynolds wanted Roy to drive her to high school. Julia refused. She wanted to take the same public bus as her cousin, June; so, with permission from Mr. Reynolds, she did. The one thing Julia agreed to do was to skip school at least once a month to go on those Friday shopping trips with her mother. Purchasing new clothes and shoes and hats and doo-dads connected Julia and her mother like nothing else did.

And then there was college. I was surprised Julia even wanted to attend. I didn't realize she had a yearning for additional knowledge. I didn't know her grades were good enough to be accepted. She didn't; she didn't; they weren't. Roy told me that Mr. Reynolds made some phone calls and called in some favors. Julia lasted for a year. Frankly, I thought she'd be home by Thanksgiving. She spent the remainder of that year moping around the house, complaining there was nothing to do, and spending her father's money on new things. When he said she could work part-time at his office, she showed some minor enthusiasm and went shopping for additional clothes.

I spent years with Julia and formed a relationship of sorts with her. I suppose she saw me as a mother figure. I looked after her and helped when I could, when I had time; but her mother kept me busy. Her parents were so tied up in their work and society obligations that Julia who was welcomed and spoiled as a baby became an afterthought as she got older. Sometimes there was an emptiness in her eyes, and I attempted to fill the emptiness with friendly conversations and little attentions because I couldn't give her the clothes and hats and shoes and doo-dads that her mother could. Those things, those doo-dads seemed to fill her life. For a time.

Chapter 11   Readjusting

In June's brain, the words could still be heard: *Kill cousin Julia; Kill cousin Julia,* and she decided to replace the ugly verb with a different one. She tried: *Love cousin Julia; Love cousin Julia,* but that was too sappy. And not quite true. Then: *Convert cousin Julia; Convert cousin Julia,* but that had a cultish air to it. The closest she could come to a satisfactory verb, one which expressed what she wished to accomplish was: *Change cousin Julia; Change cousin Julia.* But change was individual and the verb was inappropriate. How could *she* change Julia? Thinking back to her time with the therapist, she remembered that he had advised her that sometimes in life, adjustments were necessary. And if those didn't work, then, *readjust.* June found this advice helpful. She tried it out in her head: *Readjust cousin Julia; Readjust cousin Julia. Readjustment* seemed possible because when June looked up the definition, she found one of the meanings was "to adapt to a changed environment" and that might be possible. June envisioned some sentences: *Readjust our environment, and that readjustment will ease onto Julia and therefore it will be possible to: Readjust Julia.* It all made sense to June.

June began with nature. Since Julia would not go outside to nature (After the few walks they took together, she refused to go on any additional ones.) nature could be brought inside. Julia didn't like houseplants and did not want them around (June had to get rid of hers when they moved to the townhouse). Julia wasn't fond of flowers; she had no favorites, and June couldn't afford to buy them anyway, but there were ways. Just a few lovely blooms could lift one's spirits. It was late summer and most of the seasonal flowers were finished, but just outside and behind their deck, bright scarlet autumn hibiscus showed their colors. June wasn't certain she should remove any because the flowers obviously belonged to the Winchester Complex owners, but late one evening, when Julia was in the front room watching television, June took a sturdy scissors, quietly went outside, and in the dusk of the evening, snipped off three long stemmed flowering branches. She brought them inside, arranged them in a jar with water and a small bit of sugar (She had read that sugar would help cut flowers stay fresh.) and placed the jar in the middle of the kitchen table.

The following morning, June came to the kitchen to find that the flowers were closed and one of them had dropped some petals on the table. She changed the water, adjusted the jar so the sun beamed upon the closed flowers, and cleaned up the fallen petals. She hoped they would reopen before Julia appeared. She began to get the tea and coffee ready and set the oatmeal water boiling. She heard her cousin come into the kitchen, and just as she looked up from her chores ready to greet her, Julia spoke.

"What are those weeds? What are you thinking of, Julia? You know how delicate my nose is, and this is a bad time of year for fall allergies. Honestly, those are disgusting," and she walked over to the jar, lifted it up, opened the French doors to the deck, walked out, and threw the whole lot on the grass in back.

June just watched. As Julia came in, she plopped the jar down on the counter and took out the table cleaner from under the sink. She sprayed the kitchen table down. Then she wiped it, replaced the cleaner, and arranged herself on the kitchen chair. She took the remote for the television and turned on the morning news. June quietly sighed. Nature didn't seem to work. *Readjust cousin Julia; Readjust cousin Julia* she repeated in her mind. Apparently, nature wasn't the readjustment this environment needed.

On her walk that evening, June reflected. Julia didn't have many friends at the complex, and they rarely entertained. Perhaps a readjustment in their social lives would help. June though about what she could do and decided on a small dinner party. Julia should spend time with other people. A discussion about this would be required. Perhaps tomorrow morning would do. She decided to make Julia's favorite French toast in the morning and then suggest they invite some of the neighbors over. Friendship, human contact: this is what was needed to readjust Julia.

The next morning, June got up extra early, made one cup of coffee which she quickly drank, then washed and dried the coffee carafe. No coffee smell; no complaining. She even sprayed a bit of the air freshener around, then began to prepare Julia's tea and ready the French toast. When Julia came in to the kitchen, she stopped and looked at June.

"What's going on? Why French toast? Is today a special day and I forgot?"

She sat down at the table while June brought her the tea. June smiled at her. "Just thought this sounded good, and I know you like it. Why keep it for special occasions? Do you want to spread some of your marmalade on the toast or is maple syrup OK?"

"Just a small bit of the syrup," and the television went on as Julia prepared her tea.

Breakfast made, they sat down to eat and there was no noise heard except for the clinking of knives and forks and the drone from the television. June watched her cousin finish the toast and then inquired, "Would you like another piece? It will just take a minute."

"No, this is plenty. It tastes good. You go ahead and eat some more. But this is enough for me and my small frame. Thanks for making this, June."

June ignored the implied comparison of their frames, and was pleased at the thanks and the compliment and decided now was the time to bring up the dinner party.

"I've been thinking. Maybe we should have a few people in for a small dinner party. That would be fun, don't you think? We could ask Alice and Wes, and Gemma Anderson, and maybe Mr. Simmons next door. I don't think he gets out much. I could make that chicken cacciatore you like, and for dessert we could get those delicious cannoli from the bakery in town. What do you think?"

Julia finished the last bite of toast and sipped her tea before sitting back and changing the channel with the remote. Her morning game show was on. Without looking at June she said, "No."

June took a breath. In a moderated tone, attempting to sound logical and reasonable she asked, "Why not? I know you and Arnie used to give and go to many dinner parties. They can be fun, and we haven't hosted one here in well over a year."

"Right, and remember that one? Harry Wilson spilled his wine on the carpet and then his wife broke one of my best wine glasses. I know they offered to pay for the cleaning and replacement, but, really! No wonder they moved. Such a couple! Then it was a late night and I could barely get to sleep because you were cleaning and banging dishes, and the noise kept me up. Dinner parties when we were younger were fine, but now…" and Julia looked at the television and yelled, "You idiot! That's not the right answer. Honestly, where do they get these stupid contestants?"

June sat for a few minutes and then started to clean up the breakfast dishes. Maybe later or tomorrow she would bring up the subject again. When Julia was in these moods, there was no talking to her. She scraped the remains of the breakfast into the garbage and then decided, her cousin's delicate nose be darned, she was going to have another cup of her smelly coffee.

June considered. There were a couple other tactics she could try. She knew there was a way, she was sure of it, to readjust the environment's atmosphere. Once that was done, Julia would be readjusted.

***

June attempted to involve Julia in a variety of social circumstances. Events she thought would interest her cousin; invitations to be sociable and neighborly and amicable.

***

"Would you like to go to see the new movie at the County Cinemax with Alice and me?"

"Visit that filthy place? Don't you know the theater is absolutely germ-ridden? What a horrible idea! No."

***

"Julia, the local high school's senior orchestra is going to be performing at the community center. They are supposed to be very professional. Why don't we go together?"

"To hear a bunch of talentless kids on their cheap instruments? Those flutes set my teeth on edge. Ha! Count me out!"

***

"I saw a flyer for a get-together at the Winchester common room. An expert quilter is coming to show her quilts and has offered to teach anyone who wants to learn. Why don't you go with me? They are serving ice-cream afterwards. Sounds like fun."

"Sounds like a bunch of old women getting together to get free ice-cream and grow fatter. Be my guest."

***

June gave up. There would be no readjustment. The ugly verb she was trying to replace crept back. The refrain replayed in her head. This plan hadn't work. Not at all. June reconsidered, rethought, and reassessed.

Winchester Senior Complex

Free Exhibit and Lecture by

Noted quilter

Sarah Beth Summer

See her expert quilts

Learn about the history of quilting

Quilting Lessons available

Thursday in the Common Room

2:00 pm

Ice Cream will be served

Chapter 12   1955 Age 25

"Well, I guess it fits you and doesn't make you look any heavier. The tea length is fine, and I know it's in style now, but it seems a bit plain. I must admit I liked my full-length wedding dress better. Of course, I had lots of that expensive, specially imported lace on mine and yours has none. Maybe some lace, even the cheap kind, would brighten it up because it's almost too plain, but if you're happy with it I guess that's all that counts," and Julia leaned back on June's bed as she watched her cousin try on her wedding dress. Julia, having been married for over a year, considered herself an expert on everything wedding-related.

June turned one way and then another as she examined herself in the mirror in her bedroom. It was July 3, only a few weeks until her wedding, and the family was celebrating the next day's national holiday early. Julia's new husband Arnold, Uncle Albert, and Aunt Maria were all downstairs with June's parents, talking and preparing the barbeque for later. June's fiancé, Peter Coleman, was on his way, and in the meanwhile, Julia insisted upon seeing her cousin in her wedding attire and offering her expertise about the outfit and about weddings in general.

Julia's wedding dress had been fancier. And more expensive. In fact, her entire wedding had been quite an affair. She married Arnold Reynolds, the young man Uncle Albert had hired to work in his office. He turned out to be exactly the sort of husband Julia wanted. He was from an affluent family, college educated, wore classy, name-brand suits and expensive ties to work, and drove a luxury car. Arnold was gentlemanly and charming, and aware of Julia's constant attentions, but he was heedful that the attractive young woman who was flirting with him was the boss' daughter. He remained judicious and cautious with his own responses. Only when he was settled in the company and assured of his position, did he approach Albert to ask permission to date his daughter. And things proceeded from there.

Uncle Albert granted Arnold's request to date his daughter, and after a principled amount of time, he gave his consent for them to be married. In truth, he was pleased to be asked for his permission. He was further pleased to have someone he trusted, a family member now, to run the business when he retired. The wedding plans proceeded, and Uncle Albert spent whatever money was needed on his daughter's elaborate wedding: her dress, wedding attire for his wife and himself, the flowers, enormous cake, photographer, orchestra, a massive wedding reception, and all the other paraphernalia such an occasion may demand. Invitations went out to over two hundred and fifty people, and only a handful were reluctantly declined. Neither Julia nor her mother knew all those people, and the bridegroom's family was astonished at the crowd, but Uncle Albert was cognizant about those he needed to invite; favors given, favors returned. The wedding was society page news, and Julia was thrilled. So, this small, intimate wedding planned by her cousin, did not create any sort of envy in her. She was pleased to offer her expert advice and opinions.

June ignored the comments Julia made. She went to her closet, pulled out a small box, opened it, and removed the hat it held. She looked in the mirror and placed the white half-hat on her head, adjusting it to her satisfaction. She pivoted and looked at Julia bracing herself for the comment. Not that it mattered. This was what she had decided to wear. This was fitting for her wedding. This was her decision. Julia looked at her cousin, cocked her head and slowly nodded.

"It certainly goes with your dress. It is plain. I loved my long lacy veil, but this is good. Why don't you add a small veil to it? Afterwards you can remove it and just wear the hat. If you'd like, I can ask the woman who hand-made my veil to do something with your hat. There is still time to sharpen it up and make it look cute."

June smiled ruefully at the suggestion. It was what she expected Julia to say. "Thanks, but I like it just like this. I don't want a small veil. This hat fits me and my dress. Remember, my wedding will be nothing like yours. Peter and I turned down my parents' offer for a larger celebration to put the money they gave us aside for a house. We hope to get one soon, maybe in the next couple of years. That's what we want," and she turned back to the mirror readjusting the headpiece once more. She picked up a set of small imitation pearl earrings and put them on. Then a matching imitation pearl bracelet was placed on her left wrist. She turned again to face Julia.

Julia looked startled. "No gloves? I wore those lovely long lacy gloves and everybody remarked about how perfect they were. Gloves are elegant and the mark of a lady. Short gloves would be fine with your outfit, don't you think?"

June shook her head. "No gloves. I don't usually wear them and wouldn't be comfortable with them. I know we have different tastes, Julia, and this is what I want to wear on my wedding day. You said you wanted to see the entire outfit, and this is it. I like it and am comfortable in it. Did you finally pick up your suit?"

Julia was standing up to June's wedding, just as June stood up to hers. June had been the Maid of Honor, and the long pink dress she and the other three bridesmaids wore was currently peeking out of her closet where it had rested for the past year. Julia would be the only bridesmaid. Peter's closest friend would be his groomsman, and they would wear simple suits ("No tuxedoes? Really?" Julia inquired.) Julia tried to talk her cousin into a long wedding dress so she could get long formal dress too, but on this point, June was determined. So, Julia found a suit (an expensive Chanel suit) that was the shade of green June wanted. Well, not *exactly* the color June picked out but a green suit anyway, and this one better suited Julia's complexion. June didn't argue with Julia about the color. She picked her battles.

"I did. I picked it up on Friday when I went shopping. It fits perfectly now. But June, if you don't wear gloves, I can't either, and I already have the gloves that match. They are lovely. However, my hat is a bit larger than yours. I hope you're OK with that."

Julia sighed. "June, wear the gloves if you want, and the hat is fine. I'm not as fussy as you." There were several remembered tantrums during the previous wedding process. All Julia's, of course.

"Well, if you don't mind, then I will. The gloves really make my outfit, and the hat looks wonderful on me. Can you come over this week? I'll put on a fashion show for you!"

June removed her hat and jewelry and stored the items. She moved to the bed and asked her cousin to unzip her dress. As she finished putting the dress carefully away and redressed in her clothes, she nodded. "I'll try to get there. I'm working some extra hours the next couple of weeks so I can arrange to take off the four days I'd like to have for the wedding. Maybe one night this week I can get there. I'll call you when I know my schedule. OK?"

"Sure," and Julia stood up to stretch. "I took the entire week before my wedding to get ready and to relax. Of course, I never did return to Daddy's office after the honeymoon, but I didn't plan to work after marriage anyway. I needed the week before to get my hair touched up and my nails done, and I really needed a massage to relax me. It was such a hectic week! I'm glad I did all that because once we came back from our honeymoon, I was so busy seeing people and writing all those notes, I was exhausted. Didn't even have the energy to get another manicure! I'm still tired. I was so glad Mama loaned Mrs. Sampson to me to help with the writing and organizing. She did most of the cards although I did sign them. Her cursive is beautiful for a housekeeper, and there was no way I could have gotten my house in order without her and Mama's help. There were so many gifts to go through. Are you sure you can't take more days off?"

"I'm sure of it, Julia. I'm just an ordinary working person and not a busy society bee like you are. There. Everything is put away. Let's go down now and see if we can help. Peter should be here soon."

***

The wedding was exactly the way June and Peter wanted it. The weather cooperated and although it was held on a late Friday afternoon in August ("A *Friday afternoon* wedding? Are you kidding me?" was Julia's comment.), the two large fans at the Second Presbyterian Church kept the fifty guests and wedding party somewhat cool. The cake and coffee reception held in the church's lower level was brief and to the point. After greeting and thanking their guests, and toasting with the sparkling strawberry punch, the newly married couple took off for their weekend honeymoon at the downtown Palmer House Hotel. They weren't staying in the Bridal Suite because of the cost, but were perfectly content in the regular room they were able to afford for two nights.

Julia waved her cousin and her new husband off and then turned to her husband. "I hope they'll be happy. Of course, they are only traveling downtown for a couple days. Remember what a terrific time we had on our honeymoon? I bought the most wonderful outfits in Europe," and she hugged Arnold's arm as she continued to wave. Their honeymoon, a three-week trip to England, France, and Italy, was a gift from Julia's parents. Boxes filled with Julia's European finds and couture clothing were sent back to their massive apartment. The exclusive apartment in which they resided, thanks to Julia's father. He had connections. An entire year later, Julia was still unpacking things. The trip was a success, a delight. And she spoke of it often.

On their way back to the apartment, Julia continued talking about the small wedding and reception they had just left. "It was perfectly fine. And it suited June, I guess. But part of me felt sorry for her and Peter. Not sure they will ever be able to see and do all the things we did. I am so looking forward to going again. However, I wanted to do something special for them, so I sent beautiful flowers and an expensive bottle of real champagne to their room in the hotel along with a really thoughtful note. At least that will be something fun for them."

"That's a generous thing to do," and Arnold smiled at his wife.

***

The real and expensive champagne was in the room when June and Peter arrived. It was chilling in a bucket next to an effusive display of a dozen red roses. The *really thoughtful* note from Julia was prominently displayed. It read:

June and Peter,

Congratulations!

Even though this isn't Europe,

Arnie and I hope you have a wonderful weekend anyway!

XO

Julia

Chapter 13   #3 Mrs. Sampson

My sister and her husband married at the Chicago City Hall with his mother and sister and myself in attendance. Theresa altered an older dress she had by changing the sleeves, shortening the hem, and putting a bit of lace on it. Her husband splurged on a new felt hat and wore his only suit. We took the early morning bus and were first in line, so their ceremony was held at 9:30 and was over by 9:40. We celebrated by going to a nearby diner, eating eggs and bacon, and toasting the newlyweds with coffee. By noon, everyone was back at work.

That's not what happened with Julia's wedding. Although her wedding was in 1954 and not during the Depression, I was astonished at the planning and expense involved. So much hand-made Belgian lace was imported by Mrs. Reynolds that I was shocked at the amount and I was even more shocked at the price. When asked to help organize the making of the veil, I was able to get an excellent dressmaker (my sister Theresa) to work on it and to create the long veil Julia insisted on wearing. The yards of imported lace for the veil matched the additional yards of imported lace on her expensive gown which my sister also helped to alter. Theresa was nervous about working on such expensive material, but she did a fine job, and earned the money she was given. I helped my family when I could.

I was asked to the wedding and was hesitant about going, but Julia insisted I attend. Then I received an invitation, a half-hearted invitation, from Mrs. Reynolds. She probably didn't want a servant there, but I made plans to go because I wanted to see Julia married. I admit that during the ceremony, as I watched the child I partly raised walk down the aisle, some tears were wiped away. I even decided to attend the reception which was held at a downtown hotel, just to see what it was like. I tried not to look too out of place at the reception, but there were so many people there, and it was so crowded, I didn't need to worry. I was seated with some vague business associates of Mr. Reynolds, and within twenty minutes, we had run out of small talk. Over 250 guests were invited and most of them showed up to the fancy ballroom. I had never been to such a showy affair in my life and was nervous that the new (and expensive) dress I asked Theresa to make for me wasn't new or expensive enough. I needn't have worried. Honestly, no one was paying attention to me, and after the dinner, when the dancing began, I enjoyed the champagne that was offered and watched for a time before slipping out to catch the late bus home. Julia looked beautiful that day. She seemed happy then.

I still have the newspaper clipping which told of the marriage of Julia and Arnold Wagner, the promising young businessman from the office of Albert Reynolds. Arnold Wagner was a perfectly nice young man. He was attentive to Julia and courted her with flowers and small gifts. He was polite to Mrs. Reynolds, bringing her the occasional bunch of posies, and talking with her about her clubs and society business. But I always thought his strongest, most important relationship was with Julia's father. There was part of me that wondered at the convenience of Arnold falling in love with the attractive daughter of his rich and connected boss, but since Julia seemed to be pleased with it all, what did I have to say about it? Still, awfully convenient.

Two days after the wedding, Julia and Arnold left on a three-week trip to Europe where they stayed at the best hotels in England and France and Italy. When I brought the daily mail to Mrs. Reynolds, I admit to reading the postcards Julia sent, so I knew where they stayed, what they saw, and how much she shopped. Before they returned to Chicago, the boxes began to arrive. Clothes and furniture and antique doo-dads were sent to the Reynolds' house to be stored in the library along with the dozens and dozens of wedding gifts which were still wrapped in gold and silver paper and tied with mountains of white satin ribbon. The room was filled, and I wondered at all the gifts and how many were going to be useful to Julia. But the boxes from Europe kept arriving, even after they returned from their honeymoon. As I piled them up, trying to find places for them all, I thought that from the looks of it, every day in Europe was a Friday shopping trip for Julia.

They came home on a Friday night and spent most of the weekend sleeping because they were so exhausted from traveling. The following Monday morning, Arnold Warner got up, dressed, ate, and he and Mr. Reynolds left for work with Roy driving them. They did not return until almost seven o'clock that evening because there was so much work to be completed, and for weeks, the two of them kept a late schedule. Sometimes, Julia was in bed before her husband even returned to the house. She kept busy every day, meeting with designers and planning the decorating of the new spacious apartment she and Arnold would move into in a few weeks. The mountains of gifts and boxes needed to be moved to the new apartment, and I was told that for the next few months, I would be expected to help Julia get things organized. During that time, after Roy returned from driving Arnold and Mr. Reynolds to the office, he would drive Julia and me to the new apartment. Every now and then, Mrs. Reynolds would go with us. But she was busy with her own *social obligations*, as she put it, and left most of the work to us.

Their apartment was nothing like the place I grew up or the small place where Theresa and her husband and growing family lived. I knew my family was crowded in the small one-bedroom apartment, but money was tight, and even with the periodic cash I gave them, living was difficult. Not so for the newly-wed Mr. and Mrs. Wagner. I was astonished at their place. That apartment was in one of the new steel and glass buildings near the lake. The buildings were planned by some famous architect who thought "less is more", whatever that means. The apartment was on one of the top floors, had six large rooms and included three bedrooms. It made me dizzy looking out the floor-to-ceiling windows at the lake below, and I can't imagine what it cost to rent. I didn't dare ask, but I knew that Mr. Reynolds made more of his phone calls to get the place for Julia and Arnold. It was modern, too modern for me, and I was always glad to have Roy drive me back to my cozy housekeeper's quarters in the old but sturdy red-brick house I was used to. But Julia was proud of the apartment, and she and Arnold made their home there.

We spent weeks trying to organize all the gifts and European purchases, and it was a good thing that there was plenty of storage in the place. The first thing we did was unpack and organize the clothes Julia bought in Europe. Between the new stuff and her old things (She offered me some of the clothes she had, and I took them to sell because I knew nobody who could wear her size.) two full closets were filled. Poor Arnold had to store his suits and shirts in the bedroom that was used as his office. Some of the things from Europe were placed around the apartment, but others were left in their crates in the Reynold's basement storage space. I never found out what happened to those things. Eventually, we started on the wedding gifts. They had to be opened and charted in a special notebook, then put away in the cabinets or displayed. Dozens of the boxes were marked as to the contents and stored in the new apartment's extra storage space because there was no need for them. Really, what were people thinking? How many crystal decanter sets and silver trays and tea sets and engraved coffee carafes can a person use? I doubt Julia ever used most of the gifts.

The organization of it all took a long time, and after it was mostly straightened out, there were the special thank-you notes that needed to be written and sent. The customized cards had been ordered from an exclusive downtown stationery store, and once they arrived, Julia began to write them out. She tired out after writing about a dozen and asked if I would help with them. I did. She was terrible at writing, and I know my sixth-grade cursive was at least much more readable than her one-year of college penmanship. She did insist upon signing them all: *Special love and thanks from Julia and Arnold Wagner.* The postage alone was almost five dollars, and I had to stand in line forever at the post office to get the special Statue of Liberty first-class postage stamps because Julia liked their blue color. All the cards took a long time to complete because we had to double check them against the list in the notebook. It all got done, taking most of two months, and I would come back to my quarters and rub my sore writing hand with apple cider vinegar. It helped a bit.

Julia did not return to work in her father's office. She got busy with her own *social obligations* which included meeting her mother downtown on Fridays for a shopping trip and lunch. I'm unsure what else she did because she was no longer at the Reynolds' house, and I didn't keep track of her whereabouts. Once a month, she and Arnold came for a dinner. Usually, some business associates of Mr. Reynolds and Mr. Wagner were present. I always made a special dish for Julia, something I knew she would like, and I sent her home with some of the cookies with the brown-sugar icing we used to make together.

Julia always came to the kitchen to see me and give me a hug. On those nights I knew she was coming for dinner, I always wore one of the three lovely broaches she had brought as gifts to me from her European honeymoon. She got one from each of the countries they visited, and I wanted her to know I enjoyed wearing them. She would stand in the kitchen while I worked, chattering on about her life and how happy she was being Mrs. Arnold Wagner, and telling me about all the society clubs they belonged to, and the committees she was on, and how she felt so useful and was so busy. I always told her I was pleased to know that. But I watched her closely. I knew the girl, and there were things I noticed. Often her smile looked forced, and I saw dark circles around her eyes which I had never seen before. She looked thinner and bonier than she had before her wedding. And I wondered if she really was as content as in the past years when she was wearing her special professional suits and traveling in her new car to the office where her father and future husband worked together. But I said nothing and asked no impertinent questions. After my years of being with Julia and working for the Reynolds' household, I was aware of my station. I knew my place.

Chapter 14   Reassessing

Social activities in the Winchester Senior Complex continued. Mr. Simmons asked some of his neighbors, including June and Julia, over for a cocktail hour. June accepted the invitation. She went and had a wonderful time mixing with neighbors and talking with everyone. Julia stayed home but peeked out the front window to see who was attending. June and Alice enjoyed the new movie the following weekend. It was an entertaining dark comedy, and afterwards, they stopped for coffee and a donut. Julia watched a television rerun sitting in the front room. June met Mrs. Crenshaw at the high school's orchestral performance and they sat together and Mrs. Crenshaw apologized profusely for not cleaning up after her dog. The high school orchestra sounded very professional, particularly the flute section, and both women clapped heartily when the concert was completed. The afternoon was a lovely one as June walked to Winchester's common room for the advertised lecture. The expert with the quilts was both informative and instructive, and the quilts were lovely. While June did not want to learn to quilt, she discovered something about the art and thoroughly enjoyed the ice cream. She had lost a couple more pounds and treated herself. Julia did not attend but sat stonily on a kitchen chair and replaced the button on her gray cardigan as she looked for something to watch on television.

The aura in the townhouse was disturbing. Julia continued her complaints and chides, her criticism and censure, and June did her best to ignore it all as she reassessed her attempts to socialize her cousin and create a better life for them both. The women were drifting apart; living together was strained; the surrounding atmosphere was edgy, and neither roommate was happy. June kept herself busy with her activities, her books, her friends, and her walks. But she could not be absent from home all the time, and during the times she was there, Julia aggravated her and she found herself distressed.

June reassessed her finances and wondered if she could afford to live elsewhere in the Winchester Complex. Having lived in the facility for some years, she was satisfied and contented and didn't want to move to another area. The senior development was spacious and secure. It was a cheerful place to live and to keep busy with activities and friends. The townhouse itself was exceptional: generous in size, charming in design, gratifying in comfort. Julia was the impediment. Was moving to another, nearby place even an option? There were some apartment buildings in the Winchester Complex which offered living accommodations smaller in size (and in price) than the townhouse, and June wondered if she could afford the move. Perhaps she could if she went back to work part time.

She reassessed her office skills. Working twenty or so hours a week somewhere might allow her to rent one of the available apartments. But she needed to be honest with herself. In the eight years she had retired, changes had occurred in offices. She recognized the innovations that were taking place in the 1990's, but did not think she needed to keep up with them. She knew how to type (ninety words per minute!), use the copy machine, and had been learning how to send things via the fax machine. One of the younger women in the insurance office had been generous in explaining the usefulness of a computer and a floppy disk (silly name), but she retired before learning much, and she knew things had advanced and undergone additional refinements. Now, everyone seemed to have a computer and other special gadgets, and they used *The Internet* and something called the *The Google,* and June didn't understand those things. They didn't seem necessary for her current life. But she knew working in an office again would require the technological knowledge she didn't have.

She reassessed her ability to work in retail. Years ago, when both her children had been in school, June worked a part-time job during nights and weekends at a Marshall Field's store and then for some years at a Kroch and Brentano's Bookstore before taking the office job at a small insurance agency. But technology changed the retail industry too. She observed the ways stores worked now. Although it wasn't often, she did shop and wondered at the speed of the cash registers (Were they still called that?) and the implements used for credit card purchases (She didn't have a credit card…cash was king!), and she was unsure she could cope with the technology, or work the late hours, or drive the distances she would need to in her old clunker of a car. Too many changes. Too many.

More reassessment. If she couldn't afford to move, or go back to work, and wanted to continue to live at the Winchester Complex then there was only one thing left to do: wait it out. June was aware that Julia's sizeable assets and holdings were legally divided into four parts according to her trust. One-fourth would go to Julia's niece, another fourth to her nephew (June's children), an additional fourth to an arts charity that was Arnie's personal favorite, and the last fourth was June's. If June outlived her cousin Julia. Otherwise, the art charity would receive half of the assents which belonged to Julia and Arnie. It occurred to June that she needed to stay healthy and alive. Julia didn't.

A sudden clenching in June's stomach made her double over. At first, she thought she was having a stroke or a heart attack. But she sat still and reassessed her body. No, she was fine. She realized where the sudden pain came from. As she sifted through her recent thoughts, there was a hum in her prefrontal cortex and hippocampus, a rushing refrain from her gray matter, a mantra, a chant, a quaver in her soft tissue organ which became louder and more strident. June took a deep cleansing breath and tried to dismiss it, but it was as well-defined and as discernable as the high school orchestra's flute section, and the recitation continued: *Kill cousin Julia; Kill cousin Julia, Kill cousin Julia.*

Winchester Senior Complex

Announcing

Musical Entertainment

Saturday 7:00 pm

Common Room Main Hall

Gilbert and Sullivan
Senior High School Orchestra

Under the direction of

Nicholas Scriabin

Will perform a selection of classical music including:

Grieg's Peer Gynt Suite #1

And

Vaughan Williams' Fantasia on Greensleeves

Chapter 15   1960 Age 30

"…and I almost ordered the Vegas Turquoise Metallic color, but that would have taken another two months to get, and I just didn't want to wait that long, so I settled for the Seminole Red. I was anxious about not liking it, but I love the color, and Arnie said it fits my bright personality better than the turquoise. I think he's right! What do you think?"

Julia was alternately standing to look out June's kitchen window to check on her new car and turning to make sure June was listening to her which was not always the case. She was busy making lunch for the two of them and feeding her twenty-month-old daughter, Deborah, who was actively flinging bits of bread to the floor. She cleaned up the food, wiped the girl's hands, and placed a small plastic dish of cooked elbow macaroni and peas in front of Deborah. Then she placed the plate holding the chicken salad sandwich in front of Julia. She was moving as quickly as someone with a seven-month pregnancy belly could, and as Julia sat down at the table, she lowered herself into the opposite chair and sighed.

"I'm sure the turquoise would have been nice too, but the red is a lovely shade, Julia. Arnie is right. The brightness fits you. Would you like iced tea or some coffee with your sandwich?"

Julia picked up the top piece of bread on her sandwich and was picking through the innards. "Iced tea, of course. You know I don't like coffee. June, did you put onions in this? I can't eat raw ones. They just don't suit my stomach."

June got up again to pour the tea for her cousin and some water for herself. As she set the glasses down, she bent to pick up the spoon Deborah had dropped, replacing it with a clean one and answered. "No, there are no onions in the chicken salad. I know you can't eat them. Would you like some potato chips?"

"No, too fattening. Come on and sit down and talk to me. It's been too long since we were able to talk. Oh look: Deborah dropped her spoon again," and Julia, her examination complete, placed the top slice of bread on her sandwich and took a tentative bite.

June replaced the spoon, taking a couple more out of the drawer and setting them next to her. Just in case. She sat down, taking a bite of her own sandwich and fed her child some of the macaroni with another spoon. The three of them chewed for a few seconds, and then Julia spoke.

"I wish we could have gone out to lunch like I wanted to. There's a new restaurant close to Mama's house, and I wanted to try it. I could have driven, and you could ride in the car and see how wonderful it is. It has power brakes and steering, power seats and windows, and even the trunk can be opened with a button. There is air conditioning too, and it's warm enough today that I could have turned it on and let you feel how it cools. It's quite a car, June. Arnie was so sweet to get it for me, and I know it was really expensive, almost six-thousand dollars!"

June chewed her mouthful and took a large swallow of her water. Six-thousand dollars! That was almost a third of what their house cost. It was more than her husband, Peter, earned in a year! That was much more than an ordinary new car, and she wondered if Julia was lying again. She sat back and looked at her cousin.

"Julia, six-thousand dollars? Is that right? That's an awful lot of money for a car. Even a new one. Even one with air conditioning!"

"Well, this is a Cadillac Coupe Deville and Arnie got all the extras on it because the power things and the air conditioning and whitewall tires don't come with it but are special ordered and then cost more. Anyway, it was a gift for my thirtieth birthday, and we have the money so…" and Julia glanced out at the window again at the shiny new car with the sharp fins on the back and the gleaming whitewall tires. "Maybe next time we can go out to lunch. Can't you get a baby-sitter for the child?"

June looked at Julia and shrugged. "I think a lunch out will have to wait a while. I'm due in about two months, and a baby-sitter in the middle of the day is difficult to get. But I'm glad you are here, and after lunch, once I get Deborah down for her nap, I can go out and get a closer look at your car. It's a great looking car, and Arnie was generous and kind to give it to you," and she finished feeding the child while she took a few more bites of her sandwich. June would have liked to kick off her shoes and let her swollen feet breathe, but she knew Julia would complain that she was being *gauche*, currently one of her favorite words. She kept her shoes on.

The Seminole Red 1959 Cadillac Coupe Deville was the main birthday gift from Arnie, but it was not the only one. Julia also received a natural pearl bracelet and pearl earrings which matched the double strand natural pearl necklace Arnie had given her last Christmas, and which helped to expand Julia's collection of expensive jewelry. She relished showing off her possessions whenever she and Arnie went out to a dinner party or restaurant or the launch of a new museum exhibit or the opening of a theater or one of the various charity social obligations they attended. Arnie was wealthy and well connected, mostly due to the influence of his late father-in-law, Albert Reynolds, whose premature death two years ago left him in charge of the business. Arnold was positive his father-in-law would have been pleased at the expansion and diversification he had created over the past years. It was only fitting that his wife, Albert's daughter, receive the riches due her. Julia was spoiled, but justly so.

Besides, there had been sorrows for them. Julia, especially, had suffered. Her losses during their six-year marriage were profound. There was the first miscarriage just before their second anniversary which depressed Julia. Not long after they returned from a three-week cruise which was meant to help her overcome the grief from the loss, her father died and she was thrown back into a disconsolate state only to discover she was again pregnant. The second miscarriage came a couple days before June gave birth to her daughter, Deborah, and Julia was inconsolable. June's joy intensified her agony and anguish. She refused June's request to be Deborah's godmother and went through a period when she couldn't even speak to her cousin or look at her newly born niece. This lunch at June's house was only the second time they had visited in the past year and only the third time she had seen Deborah. But the joy of showing off her new car to June was reason enough to visit.

June wiped the child's hands and face and cleaned up the lunch remains as she listened to her cousin talk about the various openings and lectures and parties and dinners she recently attended. Julia was always busy with various clubs and groups, and she chattered on about different people, none of whom June knew although she recognized some of the names because they were periodically in the newspaper. She understood Julia and Arnie were society mavens. She picked Deborah up from her highchair and waited until Julia paused.

"I need to get her down for a nap. Do you want to come with us or wait here?"

Julia stood up and held out her arms for the child. "Let me carry her for you, June. Come here, Debbie, let me hold you," and to her surprise, the child allowed her Aunt Julia to carry her into the bedroom where she was readied for her nap. Julia felt a tug of maternalistic protectiveness she was not expecting as she held June's daughter for the first time ever. The little girl was tired and put her head down on her aunt's shoulder making Julia unwilling to move her to the bed.

"Let me rock her for a bit," she whispered to June, and sat down in the corner rocking chair and began to move back and forth, softly patting Deborah's back and humming a tune she didn't realize she knew. For a while, Julia closed her eyes and allowed herself to think about her lost opportunity. Opportunities. Then Deborah's mother reached over, took her sleeping child, lay her in her crib and watched as the baby moved around until she was settled. Julia, standing at the end of the bed, picked up a light blanket, covered the baby, and after a time of quiet contemplation, the two women left the room.

Together they walked out to the front porch and stood for a moment not sure what to say, what words would ease past agonies, which sounds would soothe former tribulations. There were none. Finally, Julia said, "Let me go in and get my purse, and then come out to the car with me so I can show it to you."

Julia opened the car doors, and they eased into the front seat of the Cadillac. Using her new key, she started the car and proceeded to explain the various features. She chattered on about the radio and changed the stations multiple times, turned on the windshield wipers to show both speeds, started the air conditioner, and even popped the truck open to demonstrate the ease of it. June produced the expected admiration, pronounced all the appropriate comments, and they sat in the red car small-talking their way into a farewell.

"I should get going. I'm going to stop and show Mama and Mrs. Sampson the car before I go home. We're going to dinner with some friends tonight, and then go to the London House to hear Dave Brubek, so I need to have time to get ready. Thanks for lunch, June. Next time, you should come to our place. You and Peter can have dinner, and you can bring Debbie. She would love looking out at the lake from our large windows," and Julia leaned over to air-kiss June's cheek. June eased herself and her large front out of the car and closed the door. She stood on the sidewalk and watched and waved as Julia left, her Seminole red fins turning the corner. She waited until no flame color could be seen before turning and walking into the house.

She walked to the back room to check on Deborah whose little burbling breaths could just be heard, and she smiled. She looked around the small room, wondering where they would put the second crib. Once the children were older and in school, she would need to go back to work at least part-time. She and Peter thought that they would be able to add a small third bedroom to the back of the house, but they needed to save for the construction. She sighed and went to the kitchen to clean up the dishes and begin dinner. She noticed some pieces of bread on the floor, and bending down while holding her back, she picked them up, placed them into the trash, and carried on her duties without making any noise.

Julia was headed towards her mother's house when she changed her mind. She remembered that today was one of her mother's luncheon meetings, and as much as she would love to impress the women there with her new possession, she didn't want to face their inquiries or comments or condolences regarding past losses or future plans. She was not in the mood and would see her mother another day. She turned down the busy street and drove for a while, enjoying what she knew were admiring glances from other drivers, then eased onto the expressway, and headed back to her apartment in the glass house just off the lake; to her large three-bedroom, two-bathroom unit in the sky that lacked the sound of tiny burbling breaths and survived without small pieces of bread being thrown onto the perfectly cleaned, shiny kitchen floor.

Chapter 16   Planning

A small library for tenants' use was next to several larger rooms, available for party rentals and group meetings, on the second floor in the Winchester Complex's main building. In the library, a small research section was provided. It included two full sets of encyclopedias and another partial set which was missing the *L-M* and the *X-Y-Z* volumes. Various dictionaries, three large atlases, and a heavy, out-of-date *Physician's Desk Reference* filled in the reference bookcase. Older magazines were stacked up on a magazine rack, and anyone who wished to take or supply one was welcomed to do so, and there was a continual turnover of the lot. Another bookcase was filled, with no thought to any order, with many, mostly fiction, books that various tenants had donated. A small copy machine (five cents per copy) was available for use although, when it was working, it was usually out of toner or paper or both. A computer was positioned on its own desk with a semi-comfortable chair, ready for use, although it was idle much of the time. *The Internet* and *The Google* were well beyond the cognizance of most of the Winchester Senior Complex members, although periodically a grandchild could be found using the machine with the kind of precision allotted to highly-educated, expertly-trained computer engineers. Four old but comfortable club chairs encouraged infrequent visitors with a spot to rest and read. It was to this area June came to research how to kill her cousin Julia.

During her time on the walking paths, she reviewed methods of killing in her head although she avoided thinking the words *killing* and *murder*. Instead, she substituted the term *subduing*. *Subduing Julia*. Some approaches to *subduing* had been eliminated: stabbing, shooting, drowning, choking, electrocuting. She was certain that none of these more violent methods could be executed by her due to their high-risk. She figured the perpetrator of these hands-on methods could quickly be found by the authorities, and she needed to be more subtle in her approach; her actions imperceptible; her activity undetectable; her innocence absolute. Besides, their kitchen knives were not sharp, she had no access to a gun, Julia only took showers, and the thought of actually touching her cousin to complete any necessary *subduing* actions was…well, they hadn't even hugged in decades. Electrocution seemed a possibility for a time, but the only electrical appliance Julia used on a regular basis was a hair dryer, and June was unsure how to adjust the settings to *death*.

She had short-listed three acceptable ideas: car accident, poisoning, regular accident. A car accident seemed the optimal choice until she considered the *how*. Julia kept her car in perfect condition. She took it in to the dealership at the start of every new season and had them run a diagnostic test, change the oil, and rotate the tires, all which were unnecessary at such frequent intervals. She also exchanged the car for an updated model every two years and never haggled about the cost. The dealership loved her. Each Christmas they had a large poinsettia plant sent to her with an effusive "Thank-you" card attached. Julia regifted the plant to the main office, but continued to expect the yearly flora and card as her due. June had no idea how Julia could be *subdued* in a car accident. She thought about her own almost twenty-year old car and reasoned that *she* was more likely to die that way. But she kept a plausible automobile misadventure as a possibility.

She chose a morning when there was no one at the Winchester research facility and sat down in a chair with the *P* encyclopedia volumes to research "poison." All she needed was an undetectable poison to mix into Julia's imported, expensive, loose tea from Harrington's. The substance needed to be odorless, tasteless, untraceable, and deadly. She thought about a possible autopsy finding which might point to Julia's roommate, the one who handled the tea, as the suspect, but decided that she needed to face one problem at a time. First, find the perfect poison.

She read and read but didn't take any notes. How could she? She could take no chance that her handwritten notes might be connected to research information about a deadly substance. June did find out several interesting facts.

> *Apple seeds contained *amygdalin* which could release cyanide into the blood stream. Enough seeds could kill a person. Hmmm, Julia did like apples.

> *Cyanide was absolutely a killer. It was also illegal to obtain and may have a smell of almonds. Julia's olfactory acuteness might detect this.

> *The candy-type substance marzipan tastes like almonds and could mask the taste of cyanide. Julia never ate candy.

> *Various household cleaners were poison. Julia ordered special cleaners for household use.

*Urushiol was a poison found in cashews if untreated and unroasted. Cashews were never sold this way.

June read about *Batrachotoxin* (obtained from the skin of certain small frogs in the Amazon region), *Maitotoxin* (from contaminated shellfish), *Arsenic* (a by-product of the mining process), and *Strychnine* (from tree seeds native to Australia and Asia). She cross-referenced passages and articles and looked at all three volumes, going from one to another until she felt a slight headache coming on and needed to stop. She closed the books, replaced them in the correct spaces, and sat down in the club chair which was at the back of the room. She had chosen this chair because while it was out of the sight of anyone entering the room, she had a view of the door and could quickly close her books if anyone entered. No one did. Slow day at the Winchester Complex research library.

June sat and reviewed the information. The poisoning plan did not appear to be as easy as she thought it would be. But she would keep it as a potential strategy. More research was needed, and additional sources were necessary. She should visit the library in town. June knew her car was well overdue for an oil change, and she would use that as an excuse to go there. Soon.

She sat back and rested and considered her third option: regular accident. She was unsure exactly what she meant, but she knew she needed to separate a *car accident* from other types. What would they be? She began to create a list in her mind:

*Food poisoning (Should this be listed under *poisoning*? Shouldn't she be included in this since they ate together? Could it be deadly? How much would she be affected?)

* Falling in the shower, off the back deck, in the kitchen, down the front steps (There were only three).

*Bitten by a poisonous insect (Were there any around the house? How could this be arranged?)

*Having a heavy object fall on Julia's head?

June stopped her planning. Nothing seemed to be exactly right, and it was lunchtime. She should get back to the house. Julia said she wanted a salad for lunch, and all the vegetables needed to be cut and washed and arranged just so, just exactly the way Julia wanted them positioned on her plate. And the balsamic dressing set next to the salad.

Not that Julia used much. "Watching my figure," she always said. June thought about her own lunch. No salad for her today. She was hungry. Planning made her hungry. She decided she would have a grilled cheese sandwich with some of the potato chips from the unopened bag. She didn't care if Julia would rebuke her about the calories and the fat. "That isn't good for you," she would say to June, "make another salad. Healthier!"

June got up and stretched out. She sighed. So much information swirled around in her head. This planning was stressful. Subduing Julia would take time. And probably a trip to the larger town library. Perhaps she should plan on going tomorrow after her exercise class. She left the library room and went to the staircase. Holding on to the railing, she walked carefully down the stairs to the first floor and headed to the front door. But at the bottom, she turned and counted the stairs. A landing, twelve steps and another landing. She looked up to the top. She realized that as she walked down the stairs, she held on to the railing to avoid a fall. Stairs could be dangerous. Deadly even. In fact, there was an elevator on the first floor, towards the back of the small hallway for those seniors who used a walker or wheelchair or were simply wary of a staircase. June cocked her head to one side and reflected. Then she smiled. Thoughts churned and turned in her brain as, with springy steps, she walked out the Winchester Complex main building door and strode back to the house she shared with her cousin Julia.

Winchester Senior Complex

Library Rules

Hours: 9:00 am until 7:00 pm

Winchester residents only

Return items to proper place

Do not litter

Grandchildren not allowed to use computers

Dogs not allowed

Please inform office if printer needs attention

Enjoy your Library!

Chapter 17   1965 Age 35

June rarely spoke harshly to her cousin, but this time, she voiced her views, her thoughts, her opinions, and she meant them.

A mellow sun heated the blue in the late autumn afternoon as she returned home with Daniel who had completed his morning kindergarten class at the nearby school he and his sister, Deborah, attended. They walked together towards their house where she saw her cousin Julia sitting in her new silver metallic Cadillac. The shiny car was parked, and Julia was watching as June and Daniel neared. Daniel ran ahead and up the steps of their porch while June stooped down next to the passenger side window of the Cadillac and saw Julia wiping tears away. Her first thought was that Aunt Maria had finally succumbed to one of her diseases, but that was not the case. Julia blew her nose, repositioned her sunglasses, and exited her car door. Together, the cousins walked up the steps and onto the porch where Daniel was jumping up and down trying to reach and ring the front doorbell. She got both Daniel and Julia into the kitchen where she made Daniel his lunch, Julia a cup of tea ("Tea BAGS! Really?"), and poured herself a glass of water. Wiping her son's face as she sat down across from her cousin, she looked at her and waited for the explanation the for the visit.

"No, there is nothing wrong with Mama. She's fine. Perfectly fine," replied Julia to the repeated inquiry. "I needed to talk to you. I just drove here from Mama's house because we had a massive argument, and I had to leave. Mama just needs to stay out of my business. She's been listening to those old women she calls *friends* who run their mouths about things which are none of their business. She listens to them and believes them, and this time they were gossiping about ME. The argument was about me and my friends. Or one friend in particular," and she delicately wiped her eyes with a tissue from the box June had placed before her. "I am just angry and upset."

"And that would be because…?"

Julia opened her mouth to say something and then shut it. She glanced at June, then tilted her head towards Daniel who was dipping the remainder of his sandwich into his milk and squishing it in his hand. She looked back at June and cocked her head to the other side.

"Little pitchers, June. Isn't Danny going to take an N-A-P soon?"

June looked at her son and sighed. "Daniel, are you finished?

OK, let's wash your hands and then you can have a quiet time in your room. You can look through some of your books there," and ignoring the squealing and protestations from the five-year-old, June got her son down from his chair to complete the tasks. "I'll be right back," she called to Julia. She escorted Daniel to the bathroom and then into his room where she settled him in his bed placing half a dozen books around him. She opened one and set it before him, encouraging him to look through it. She leaned down to kiss his forehead, then left, closing his bedroom door part way, and returned to the kitchen.

She watched as Julia wiped her eyes and blew her nose. Then she sat down at the table, expelled a single sigh, and looked expectantly at Julia. "What happened?"

"I went to visit Mama today, and she started in on me practically the moment I entered the house. Yesterday she had one of her clubs over for a luncheon and apparently some of the women in the Garden Club were also at the Business and Arts Club's dinner last week. I was there, but Arnie was in New York on a business trip, so a friend of mine, Joseph, picked me up, and we went together. We are simply friends, and there is nothing wrong with us attending the events at the club, but Mama's friends made a big deal out of it, upsetting Mama and causing us to argue. Really, it's just ridiculous." And Julia wiped her eyes again.

June offered her more tea and while she was wiping out her cup and reheating the water, she asked some questions. She knew her cousin did not always tell the complete story and suspected there was more to this one.

"I haven't heard about this friend, Joseph, before. Is he a new friend? Is he Arnie's friend too? Is he married? Why was there such a fuss? What else was going on? Other things must have happened, Julia. There's more to this story. I can't imagine why there would be talk unless something else happened."

"Well, Arnie doesn't really know Joseph, but I'm sure I've mentioned him. I don't remember. I might have forgotten to tell Arnie we were going to the dinner together. No, he's not married. At least, not now. He and his wife are divorced. Or at least separated and waiting for a divorce. I think his wife is in Florida. Ex-wife. I don't really know. And it doesn't matter. We're just friends. Those old women made it sound like the two of us are having an affair. So nonsensical!"

June sat down at the table. "Julia, why are you so upset? It seems there is another reason. If this whole thing was nothing, then why did you and Aunt Maria argue?"

Julia took a sip of the tea. She looked down at the cup and then pushed it away. She sat back against the slats of the chair and sighed and was still again. June waited for her to explain.

"Joseph and I have been to various events together before. Once or twice, we went to dinner when Arnie was away for business and some of those old women saw us together and jumped to conclusions. Mama threatened to tell Arnie about Joseph and me. She would only cause problems, and I told her she would, but she claims this was not the first time she heard about the two of us, and not the only time someone mentioned we were seen together at something. It's all nonsense, of course, and gossip, but one thing led to another, and we were talking loudly, and Mrs. Sampson came it to see what was going on, and..." her voice trailed off, and she didn't look at June but down at her hands.

"So, there is more to this story than you are saying. It sounds like you are seeing a lot of this Joseph, and Arnie does not know about it. Julia, *are* you having an affair?"

"The whole thing is complicated, June."

"How is it complicated?"

Julia didn't answer. She twisted her hands around each other and didn't speak, so June asked again.

"How is this complicated? Are you and Joseph having an affair? The answer to my question is *yes* or *no*. And if you are, what is wrong with you? You're acting guilty, and if it seems like that to me, then it must to other people too. What's going on? Why are you going out with this man when Arnie is not at home? You came here because you're upset, but if you are fooling around, then you must know I am not on your side."

"*Fooling around*...such a stupid phrase. I simply have been to a few events with Joseph. He is interesting and fun, and Arnie is on business trips so often that I am bored. Joseph and I happen to belong to some of the same clubs, and it's convenient to go to events together. We've gone to dinner a few times, and Mama is making a big deal about this, and her stupid friends are encouraging her. I just wanted to see if I could talk to you about this, but you don't understand. How could you? You're stuck in this four-room house with two kids and a part-time job as a store clerk, and you and Peter never do anything exciting for fun. You can't understand what my life is like," and Julia stared at June, goading her into an argument, waiting for her reply.

June said nothing. She picked up her water and took a swallow and set the glass down. She waited for a few seconds before speaking.

"No, Julia, I don't even pretend to understand your life of clubs and social events and dinners and plays and museums. And you are right about the fact that we have a four-room house and two kids and I work a part-time job at Marshall Field's and Peter and I rarely go out. We're busy with our family and with working and trying to save the money to build another bedroom on the back of this four-room house so our kids don't have to squeeze into the same room forever. But I don't want to see you and Aunt Maria arguing. You are good at changing the topic and never answered the question I asked. If you are having an affair, you know it's wrong. Arnie is a hard-working man who has given you whatever you want: cars and trips and gifts of all sorts. I'm done lecturing you. I just want you to be happy, and I can see you're not. Stop fighting with Aunt Maria. She isn't well, and I worry about her. I guess you're right about one thing: we don't understand each other's lives," and she stopped talking and waited.

Julia didn't speak. She allowed June's words to wrap around her thoughts, testing their validity, gently squeezing out any accuracy. For an infinitesimal flow of time, truth was present. They sat at the kitchen table, a lawn mower thrumming in the background and distant traffic noises stirring the afternoon air until finally, Julia looking up, took another tissue, and blowing her nose gave June a wry smile.

"No, I suppose we don't understand each other's lives, June. And I guess you're right. I don't want to upset Mama. I know she's not well, and I don't want to add to her problems. I'll call her once I get home. Arnie *is* a good husband. He does spoil me, and I know the trips he takes are important. He has asked if I wanted to accompany him on some, and I've always said *no*, but maybe I'll rethink that. I might need to rethink a few friendships too. We were considering not rejoining the Business and Arts Club once our membership is up for renewal. There are lots of other clubs we could join and enjoy together, and I should investigate them. Arnie will be home tomorrow night, so I guess we could talk about it then."

There was a silence in the kitchen, and June looked at her cousin and nodded her head in agreement. This topic was finished. The subject was changed, and the two women conversed about other things. A tacit truce was reached.

This was the closest Julia would ever come to admitting she hadn't kept to the marriage vows she made more than eleven years earlier. June never brought it up again, but shoved her cousin's possible (probable?) infidelity to the back of her mind. It would not surface again for years. Not until she found herself walking the path around a small lake, making a *Pro/Con* list on a magic blackboard in her head.

Chapter 18   #4 Mrs. Arnold

You would think that living for years in the same house with people would lead to some sort of friendship, but that's not necessarily true. Mr. and Mrs. Reynolds were not my friends. Mr. Reynolds was a busy man who was working a great deal and rarely home, and while he was always polite to me and decent in his treatment of me, I knew my place. His wife was mostly the same although we had more interactions, especially when it came to Julia. Mrs. Reynolds was the girl's mother, but it seemed to me, she didn't relish the role. From the first time Julia cried as a baby and I picked her up, Mrs. Reynolds was relieved to let me handle her; was pleased that there was someone there to feed and clean her and do the unpleasant stuff. Of course, she would sometimes read to her and rock her, and as Julia got older, there were times when they seemed to be a bit closer. I know they enjoyed their Friday shopping trips and the holidays with the decorating and present wrapping, and the entire year of wedding planning brought them a chummier relationship, but Mrs. Reynolds was one of those women who wanted children but not the duties that came with them. I often considered that it was lucky she had just the one.

The lady of the house and me had our own places, and once my tasks were completed, I would disappear into my rooms and keep to myself. Sometimes I visited with a few of the neighborhood housekeepers I got to know, and we would go to a restaurant for a meal, grateful that someone else made it. Now and then I would visit my sister, Theresa, and her husband and their children. Sometimes I would even stay overnight at their house and sleep on their lumpy sofa and wish my life had taken a different path, but mostly, I was settled in my life at the Reynolds' house. I became friends with Roy, the family and business automobile driver and his wife, and through them got to know a few more people, so I wasn't without friends. But Mrs. Reynolds and I couldn't be called *close.* We didn't sit together in the darkened parlor talking or listening to the radio or enjoying tea together as we watched the television (when they got one). At least not until Mr. Reynolds died and Princess was gone. Then the loneliness which I was used to seemed to burden her, and the relationship between us shifted. We could be called *companions* since I sometimes felt like a family pet who was periodically called upon to sit at her mistresses' feet and just be there. I accepted the life I had and tried to make the best of it. And, if sometimes, one of the pure silver doo-dads that were crowded into the many curio cabinets decorating the place found its way to the pawn shop I regularly visited, well, the money I put away was aimed for good use. I needed to prepare for my future, to feather my nest, to ensure I wouldn't need to totally rely upon Theresa and her family to take care of me in my old age. The wealth of the Reynolds was my pension fund.

After Mr. Reynolds died, Julia, for a time, would visit her mother once a week. That didn't include the Friday shopping trips, so I guess they saw each other a couple times a week. There were times, on a weekend, Julia and her husband, Arnold, would come for a dinner. Even though I was to have Saturday afternoons and Sundays off, I was sometimes asked to stay and to cook. I did this happily because when I did, Mrs. Reynolds would find a way to thank me, and that way included some extra cash in my pay envelope. I stayed and made dinner and cleaned up. I was glad to see Julia because the girl was always kind to me. She never forgot my birthday or a holiday, and on Mother's Day, when she visited Mrs. Reynolds, she always had a little gift of some sort for me. I have an entire chest filled with sweaters and shawls and scarves that I will never wear, but I can't gather the gumption to sell. Yet. I suppose one day I will. They are of the best quality and will bring a good price at the pawn shop. Pension keepings.

For the first couple years, Julia and Arnold seemed satisfied with their marriage. Then, just before their second anniversary, Julia announced she and Arnold would be parents. I was delighted for her and hoped she would be a more competent mother than her own. But she lost that baby, and for months, was awfully sad. I know. I was sent to her apartment to care for her afterwards. Roy would take me there, and I would sit with her and try to get her to eat and rub her back to try and ease her into a nap. I would make dinner and cook and do what little cleaning her own housekeeper didn't get done. In the early evening I would get picked up by Roy and returned to the Reynolds' place where I reported on her situation. Mrs. Reynolds didn't go herself to console Julia, because that wasn't her style. In fairness, she did accompany me twice, but she wasn't such a consolation, and Julia, at the end of second visit, told her *to go home to your stupid clubs and leave me alone.* She did.

I continued the visits daily for a week and then a couple times a week until one day when I came, Julia was already up and dressed and told me she was going to resume her own club meetings and activities and plan for a vacation. That was a good sign, I thought. That day, before I left, Julia handed me a large package and told me to do something with it, that she didn't need it. I set it to the side and didn't look in it until

Roy drove me home. When I saw the tiny lemon yellow and soft green colored baby outfits, the wee socks and shoes and several bibs which looked hand-made and all very expensive, I figured that this was the result of one of her Friday shopping trips. I thought to put them away; to save them for another time and then return them to her. They were lovely and Julia was still young. At home, I went to my rooms and opened the chest which held Julia's gifts. I put the package under the last shawl she gave me, the one which came with a bit of paper explaining that it was a real Kashmir Pashmina shawl. It was cushiony and delicate, and nothing I would ever wear, but it covered the baby clothes and was as soft as a mother's hug.

After that, Julia and Arnold went on a special cruise. They were gone for weeks, and during that time, Mr. Reynolds worked long hours at his office. He had been taking it a bit easy and was home often because Arnold was doing most of the work. "Good man. Business is booming. He's got plenty of new ideas," is what I heard him say to Mrs. Reynolds. But with the Wagners gone on a trip, there was more work for him. I'm not saying that's what brought on the heart attack, but it wasn't too long after Julia and her husband returned from their cruise that it happened. A sad time indeed. And Julia was miserable. Mrs. Reynolds was too, but it was Julia who worried me. When I saw her, she looked thin and pale and drawn. I reflected at her condition and was right. After the funeral, she came over to help her mother sort through her father's clothes, and she told her, and then me, that she was expecting again. Sadness mixed with joy.

We all held our breaths, and for some weeks everything seemed good. Julia's cousin, June was expecting her first baby too, and there was talk about how the babies would be brought up close, just like Julia and June. I was waiting for the right time to dig out the baby things and give them back to Julia, sure she would be grateful I had held them safe, but they weren't to be used. Just around the time June's daughter, Deborah came into the world, Julia lost her second one, and this time there was a real change in her. She hardened. She grew unkind. At least I thought so. She never changed towards me, but I heard her sharpness to her mother and to June and a few times to Arnold. I thought this was a temporary hurting, but maybe not. She refused to be the godmother to Deborah and wouldn't attend the doings at the church or afterwards at June's house. I don't think she even saw the child until Mrs. Reynolds told her she was being selfish. They had a big to-do about this, and Julia was not seen at the house for weeks after. Then she did show up, but I knew that the hidden baby clothes would remain under that soft shawl.

I'm sure Julia didn't mean for me to find out about her third loss, and I don't think Mrs. Reynolds ever knew about it. I happened to be at Julia's apartment. I was asked to come and make a special dinner for some important guests Arnold was entertaining, and I had been driven there by Roy three days in a row. The first day I found Julia in the bathroom, weeping and bleeding. I saw what she cried over and wanted to call the ambulance, but she stopped me. We called a taxicab, and I went with her to her doctor's office where she insisted that whatever needed to be done be accomplished there and refused the hospital. Because the whole thing had such an early start, the doctor agreed, and I took her home later that day and put her to bed, and called Mrs. Reynolds to make up an excuse about staying overnight because there was so much to be done. Julia made me promise not to tell anyone, and I didn't. Apparently not even Arnold knew, but that wasn't any of my business. I kept quiet and when he came home, I served him dinner and explained that his wife had gone to bed early with a sick headache. They slept in separate bedrooms that night, and I made do on the living room couch. As far as I know, no one except the two of us knew about the third baby. I waited for a month or two before digging out the bitsy yellow and green outfits and taking a walk to the pawn shop. This time the money I got didn't go into my pension savings. Instead, I bought some toys with it and took them to my nieces and nephew the next time I went. At least some children got some use from the clothing.

Julia and Arnold were always busy. They belonged to various clubs and ate out often and gave dinner parties. I cooked for the parties and was put in charge of hiring a staff to serve when the crowd was large. In this way I was able to help my own nieces who I hired and trained much the same way I did with their mother in the early years with the Reynolds. Besides the clubs and dinners and social events, Julia and Arnold traveled. They went on trips and cruises a couple times a year. Whenever they traveled, Julia brought back something for me from the places they visited. She was thoughtful in that way, and I appreciated her gifts even as they crowded my own small curio cabinet. Money seemed to be plentiful, and besides the fanciest clothes and jewels, each year she had a new automobile, always a costly one with lots of extras on it and usually the red color she liked. I guess the clubs and trips and necklaces and cars were the doo-dads that became Julia's children.

As both Mrs. Reynolds and Julia grew older, the closeness they once had disappeared. They would argue. Sometimes I would hear them as I worked in the kitchen or cleaned the upstairs, and once or twice, the shouting got so loud that I poked my head into the parlor thinking that the yelling was not good for Mrs. Reynolds. One of the biggest fights they had was about the dog.

Mrs. Reynolds got a dog. It was a suggestion from one of her friends in the Garden Club, and she decided that it would be a good idea. She got a poodle dog. Silly name, if you ask me, but then she seemed happy with it, and when it was small, it was a cute thing. She kept its fur sparkling white, put a pink ribbon around its neck, and named it *Princess*. Of course, either Roy or me had to care for the thing, and when I finally told Mrs. Reynolds I would not clean any of its messes again, she asked around and got the thing trained. It was better after that, and it took to Mrs. Reynolds, always curling up close to her and nudging her to be petted. It would sometimes come into the kitchen thinking to be fed. At first, I gave it some bites, but after I had to clean up the mess it made from a sick stomach, I stopped that. The dog and me got along for the two or so years it was there, but I wouldn't say we were the best of pals. We tolerated and mostly ignored each other. The problem came when Julia was there. She didn't like the dog, and it didn't like her.

I saw Julia being mean to the animal. When she came in the house, the dog growled until Mrs. Reynolds told it to "Hush, Princess!" A couple of times, Mrs. Reynolds said she saw Julia kick it. Now I'm sure it was not a real whole-hearted kick, but Julia didn't want the dog around her, and I'm believing she moved it out of her way with her foot. Just guessing. Julia was always telling her mother to get rid of it. She argued it might have fleas or worms, or all sorts of diseases and could pass them along to whoever visited. But Mrs. Reynolds had grown fond of the thing and ignored Julia. Until that one day.

I remember it was a windy spring day because Mrs. Reynolds wanted the sheets hung out on the back line in the air and sun. I did that, but had to go out twice to replace the end of one on the line because the wind blew off the clothespins. I came back in and heard a sound in the front. It was Julia, driving up in her new red car, and when Princess saw her, she began to bark and growl.

"Shut up, dog!" yelled Julia, and this time, as I went to get the door, I saw her push it open, pushing Princess out of the way, and it was not a gentle push. "Mama, I'm here. Hello, Mrs. Sampson. Wow, is it windy!" and as she came in, she went to the dining room and removed her coat and took off the scarf she had covering her hair, placing them across a chair. "Where's Mama?"

"I'm here, Julia. Stop screeching and come into the parlor," and that's where Julia went.

I didn't look for Princess because she had run to the back of the house, and I knew Julia and her mother would want tea, so I went to the kitchen to get it ready for them. I took the tray in, filled with the tea makings and some of the shortbread cookies I had just finished and left them to their discussion. The sheets in the back were dry, so I walked out and began to unfasten and fold them. I came inside to the arguing.

Now, I have a few headscarves myself. I bought them at the Woolworth's and they are perfectly fine for wearing on a windy or cold day. But I know I didn't pay much for them. I didn't know until that day, what a *Hermes* scarf even was, and when I found out the cost of one, I was shocked. That much for a piece of cloth? And not even wool. Mrs. Reynolds and Julia were yelling at each other while Julia held the remains of a scarf Princess had gotten hold of and chewed up. The dog was nowhere to be found. Lucky for her. I think Julia would have knocked it in the head with her shoes which were also expensive.

"Mama, get rid of that animal. Look at this! It's the first time I've worn it and your disgusting animal destroyed it. Why do you even have it? It's a dirty creature and obviously not trained!"

"Princess didn't mean anything. She had no idea it was so expensive, and she is a pet and a comfort to me, Julia. She is here and you rarely show up, and when you do, there is always something we argue about! I'll get you another scarf if that's what you want!"

"I want that creature gone. In fact, I won't be back until it is. Call and let me know which of us you prefer, Mama. I'm leaving," and Julia grabbed her coat and purse and what was left of the Hermes scarf.

When she got to her car, she zoomed away so quickly, I expected to hear a crash. But Mrs. Reynolds and I head a different crash in the parlor, and we rushed in to see that Princess had gotten into the tea set and the shortbread cookies, making a mess, and causing Mrs. Reynolds to shout at Princess who ran to the back of the house and stayed there for hours.

We both cleaned up the tea, and I took the broken pieces of the cups and saucers to the kitchen. They were beyond repair, and I was told to just thrown them out. Mrs. Reynolds said she was going to her room to lay down. I went to the kitchen to get a sponge and finish cleaning the parlor rug. Princess hid. It was a sad day for everyone.

Julia did not call or come over for most of a month. Princess never regained the favor of Mrs. Reynolds, and about three weeks later, she asked Roy to take Princess and find a good home for her. I never asked Roy what he did with the dog, although once when I was at his house for a Sunday supper, I saw a dog looking very much like Princess in the back yard two doors down. I watched as two girls came out and threw a ball to the dog who fetched it, and they played for a long while. The dog was a dirty white, and there was no pink ribbon surrounding its neck, but it seemed happy to jump around the yard with the girls, and I thought that if it was Princess, that place with those girls was a better home for her.

Julia and her mother made up, and continued their monthly Friday shopping trips and the occasional visits. But something had happened to Mrs. Reynolds. She lost interest in her clubs and shopping and would sit for hours and stare out the window. Sometimes she wouldn't get dressed until noon and only then, after I said something to her, would she put on the same clothes she wore the day before. She forgot simple things like where she put her purse, or to tie her shoes, or to comb through her hair. She didn't have much of an appetite and her clothes started to just hang on her. I encouraged her to eat the meals I prepared for her, but she continued to lose weight. She became more and more forgetful and seemed sad much of the time.

It was during this time she wanted me to sit with her in the parlor to listen to the radio or to drink tea and watch television, so I would usually join her there. I watched as she turned on the television and sometimes her head would just nod and her eyes would close, and then she'd start awake and ask, "What was that?" That was the time, it seemed to me, I took the place of Princess. I was the substitute companion. But she remained kind to me, and sometimes, because of her forgetfulness would pay me three times a month instead of the usual two, and I just figured that the extra cash was payment for being her doggie substitute. Pension payment.

Chapter 19   Delaying

Julia had an accident. Not a car accident, a regular accident. One that was not planned by June. In fact, June was not around when it happened. She had been at the Winchester Complex's library room researching the subduing of her cousin, reading about *Batrachotoxin* and *Cyanide;* reflecting about how she could afford to get her old car checked out so she would not have her own car accident; thinking about making Julia's healthy salad and her own unhealthy grilled cheese sandwich. She walked home, considering whether she should go to the town library in a day or two to do further research, but as she got closer to the townhouse she shared with Julia, she noticed unusual activity. An unfamiliar car was parked crookedly next to the curb, the front door of the townhouse was open, and voices could be heard coming from the inside.

"Well, Mrs. Wagner, I don't think it is broken, but you really do need an x-ray to determine that. An ambulance can be called and would be here in just a few minutes," and June saw a man she knew was one of the residents, a retired doctor, Dr. Bennett, bending down to look at Julia's right ankle which was elevated on a kitchen chair and wrapped with frozen vegetable bags. Mrs. Nowak, the office manager, Mr. Simmons, the next-door neighbor and June's friends, Alice and Wes were all standing around, appearing somber and staid, shaking, or nodding their heads.

"Nonsense," Julia insisted., "An ambulance is unnecessary. When June gets home, she can take me to get an x-ray. Where on earth is she? Honestly, she said she was going for a walk and that was hours ago! Maybe one of you could go around the neighborhood and look for her. I…" and, before Julia could complete her instructions, June stepped forward to present herself: The Truant.

"What is going on? What happened, Julia? Are you OK?"

Julia barked at her. "What do you think? What does it look like? No, I'm not OK! I had a terrible accident! I fell outside of Mr. Simmons' house, and Alice and Wes brought me here. They called the main office because *you* were nowhere to be found. Here I am, lying on the sidewalk, injured and in pain, and you are gone. And I am alone. And suffering!"

June commented, "Well, I'm here now. Let's see what needs to be done."

She turned to the doctor, asked questions, and after a brief discussion with him, and Alice and Wes, and Mrs. Nowak, it was decided to get Julia into her own car (*"Your* car? I would sooner get in a garbage truck!" was Julia's response when June said she would move her car from the garage.) and drive her to get an x-ray. Julia refused the ambulance, refused Wes' offer to drive her, told Mrs. Nowak to quit asking if she wanted something to drink, yelled at June to "Get moving!", and eventually, with all the pageantry of moving a rare and expensive museum painting from one building to another, Julia was deposited, among pillows and blankets, into the back seat of her own car with June acting as chauffeur.

The trip to the emergency care center, the location Dr. Bennett advised June to go ("No, Dr. Bennett, thank you, but you do not need to go along. June should do this," instructed Julia.) was miserable. For both June and Julia. Dr. Bennett had called ahead and informed them that Julia was on her way, and two attendants were waiting with a wheelchair when the car arrived. Julia, without a fractured ankle, tended to be disagreeable, but Julia, with a fractured ankle, was worse. And her ankle was fractured.

It was a slight fracture. No walking on it for at least four weeks and she was instructed to keep it elevated. A splint was necessary, and after it was removed, Julia would need to wear a walking boot and use a cane. Because of her age, physical therapy would be required. The healing time would be eight to ten weeks. Eight to ten weeks! Possibly longer. Julia complained. June sighed.

Julia talked about her accident ("My catastrophe when you were nowhere to be found ..." she would begin.) continually. She explained that she went outside to look back at the townhouse because she heard an explosive sound on the roof ("...and I thought the ceiling was going to fall on top of me!") and wondered what it was. June was not there to look for her, so she had to do it herself ("...and missed all my morning programs!"). She couldn't see, so she walked over in front of Mr. Simmons' house wondering if the noise was on *his* roof, and stepped back to look up. That was when she tripped. She knew, she just knew her ankle had been damaged as soon as she fell backwards. She twisted her right ankle and fell directly on her backside ("It's a wonder I didn't break my spine!") which knocked the wind out of her. She sat there for a few seconds ("I am sure it was close to fifteen minutes before anyone even came to see if I was hurt!") and began to scream for help. Mr. Simmons came out of his house, but he could do nothing ("Useless as a screen door on a submarine!"), so he went next door to Alice and Wes to obtain their help. They came over and between them, helped move Julia into the house while Mr. Simmons called the main office. Mrs. Nowak ("Disgusting woman with bad breath!") drove over bringing Dr, Bennett. The rest of the story June knew by heart. She heard it repeatedly.

Julia complained. She groaned and grumbled. She moaned and fretted. She bellyached and whined. And June put up with it. She brought her cousin her imported Harrington tea, the New Zealand Manuka honey and the thinly sliced, freshly cut lemons. Meals were served on a tray while Julia watched television, mumbling at the stupidity of the contestants on her game shows between bites. When Julia dropped the television remote, June needed to pick it up. Once the injured foot was freed of wrappings, June carried in a small bucket filled with Epsom salts and tepid water to soak the injured ankle. She dried it too. And then, cautiously, gingerly, rubbed it with a special lotion Julia sent her to buy. She also purchased the cane Julia needed, but then she returned it because Julia did not like it. It was "…too dark in color! My God, don't you have any sense? Get a light oak colored one!" June placed the flowers sent to Julia by Mrs. Nowak in the office, Dr. Bennett, Alice and Wes, and even the car dealership (They called because she missed her seasonal appointment.) on the back deck because they were lovely, but "…the smell makes me sick. Get those things away from here." Such was Julia's directive.

June did these things because now she knew. This entire regular accident was only a delay. A temporary delay. A brief interruption. A plan was taking form. A strategy was being invented. This fortuitous misfortune had happened once. Something similar could very well happen again. After all, Julia had just proven herself careless. Once someone older falls, they often fall a second time. There might be a delay in the plans due to Julia's first accident. But once she was up and about again, using her preferred light oak colored cane, limping, and learning to adjust, who knew what might occur? What might transpire? What additional tragedy could befall an elderly person? What dreadful circumstance might develop? And accidents do happen.

Chapter 20   1970 Age 40

"What is this called again?"

"It's called a *Harvey Wallbanger*," answered Julia, "It's made with Galliano liqueur. Do you like it?"

"It's certainly sweet," said June as she took another sip. "I couldn't drink two of these. Of course, I'm not much of a drinker anyway. Peter?" she called to her husband. He was sitting next to Arnold, and they were both drinking a beer. "Do you want to taste this?"

"No thanks, this Old Style is just fine," and he took a swallow from the can and the two men continued to watch *Lassie* on television with Deborah and Daniel who were both watching the television and playing the new *Battleship* game they had just unwrapped.

Christmas was two days past, and the children had opened all the presents from the family, including the ones from Aunt Julia and Uncle Arnie. But when they arrived for a post-Christmas dinner at the glass-and-steel apartment by the lake, their aunt had additional gifts for them, and they delightedly tore off the wrappings. Daniel was told he could not throw the Nerf football in the apartment even though the box claimed "World's First Official Indoor Ball", and Deborah said she loved the music box whose ballerina twirled when it was opened, but those gifts couldn't be played. The *Battleship* game would keep them occupied, and they read through the instructions and began to play.

Outside, the snow quietly fell, and it was cozy. Julia had prepared the Sunday evening supper herself, and the sloppy-joe Manwich sandwiches filled up the men and the children, while Julia and June enjoyed using the new cheese fondue pot. After eating, the dishes were piled in the sink. June wanted to wash them immediately, but Julia insisted they toast the holiday first with the new drink she made herself. They sat at the dining room table and talked as the television in the other room occupied everyone else.

"I'll bet Aunt Maria and Mrs. Sampson would like this drink," commented June as she took another sip. "I wish they would have come. I even called this morning to see if they had changed their minds, but your mother said that snow was due, and they would just stay in and stay warm. I told her we could pick them up in a warm car and take them home in one, but they didn't want to be out in the cold. I think Aunt Maria was afraid if falling, even though I assured her we would walk with her. Too bad."

"Mama doesn't go many places these days and has practically no company. She seems content just watching television or listening to the radio. I ask Mrs. Sampson about her all the time, and I guess they both are satisfied with each other's company. So many of Mama's friends have passed away or moved to Florida. Speaking of which… how are your parents doing? Florida is so much warmer than here; I am positive they don't miss the Chicago weather. Do you have plans to visit them soon?"

June pushed the tall ice-filled glass away, leaving the last few sips in it. She didn't really like the drink, but didn't want to annoy her cousin with the truth, so she got through most of it. She would really prefer some coffee, but knew Julia would not be making any. June wasn't a tea drinker, but if that were offered, she would take it. Really, anything would do to get the taste of the Harvey Wallbanger out of her mouth. She shook her head and spoke.

"No. No plans to visit this year. I would like the kids to know their grandparents and spend time with them, and I would love to see them, but right now we have to make do with monthly phone calls and letters. They seem to like their apartment complex, and when we visited last summer, we all liked the weather there, but it was so warm. Rain most afternoons, and while the kids liked the pool, I was always telling them to not splash so much because of all the older folks around. Peter and I are saving for the new car, and once we get it, we might be able to drive down in another year. Maybe even at the end of this next summer. Depends on how Peter's new job goes. I'm earning more money now at the office, and of course, working full time helps, so we'll see."

Julia nodded and finished her drink. "Do you want another one? No? Sure? OK, can I get you anything else?"

"Water is fine, and why don't we wash up those dishes? We can talk while cleaning up."

"I can leave them for Mrs. Wilson to do in the morning," and Julia leaned back in her chair.

"Why? They will be all sticky and hard to clean then. Come on, Julia, I'll wash. I don't know where they go, so you can dry and put them away," and not giving her cousin a chance to refuse, June stood up, took her glass with her, and walked into the kitchen.

Julia reluctantly followed with her empty glass. She considered making another drink, but she had one (or two) before June and her family arrived, and another would make three (or four), and they were sweet. Too much sugar. She decided not to indulge. June expertly organized the dishes and pans to be cleaned and looked around for an apron.

"Is there an apron around?"

Julia shrugged. "I don't know. Mrs. Wilson has some but I think she brings them with her and doesn't leave them here."

June took a dishcloth and wrapped it as far around her waist as it would go and began to wash the pile of dishes. They worked in silence for a few minutes, June washing and scrubbing and Julia half-heartedly drying.

"Really, these could be left to soak. What's the sense in having a housekeeper three days a week if there is nothing for her to do?"

June glanced at her cousin. "Three days a week? Why? I can't think this house is that dirty. Does she also cook for you?"

"Yes, she usually makes meals on Monday and Wednesday. There is plenty left over for me, and Arnie is rarely home before eight or nine. He grabs dinner somewhere or has business meetings, and the rest of the week, we go out. We rarely eat here together, so daily meals aren't necessary. I'm often out for a lunch meeting with some of my clubs or committees, and once a month Mama and I meet downtown to shop and lunch. At least we did. I do try to get to the house for a visit a few times a month, and Mrs. Sampson always prepares a great lunch. I miss her cooking. Mrs. Wilson does a decent job, but I grew up with Mrs. Sampson's way of cooking and baking, and I do miss it. I suppose you cook at home all the time," and Julia reached up to put the plates into the cabinet.

"I do, but I have to plan carefully now that I'm working full time. I don't get home until around 4:30, so I've been relying on the pressure cooker for making quick meals. It's been great."

"How is the new job? So glad I don't have to work."

June took a deep breath. "It's fine. The other two women are friendly, and the day goes by quickly. I'm learning more about the insurance business, and both Sandy and Evelyn are great about answering my questions. We're working out a holiday and vacation schedule for this next year over the next few days, so that should be helpful in planning things. I just hope the weather isn't so bad that the buses run slow tomorrow morning. That sometimes happens. I told the family that we're going to eat light this week, and I'll bake a ham and have cheesy potatoes for New Year's Day. Are you sure you and Peter don't want to come?"

Julia took the pan and wiped it and set it on the counter. She wasn't sure exactly where it went and Mrs. Wilson might need it tomorrow.

"Thanks, but the club will have its usual dinner/dance for New Year's Eve, and Arnold and I know it will be a late night. We're staying at one of the downtown hotels for a couple days, and then meeting some friends New Year's Day at night. Are we done here? The rest will just dry by themselves. Come into the bedroom. I'll show you the new dress I bought. It's lovely. It's a Pierre Cardin beaded gown, and I'm sure no one at the club will have anything like it. It fits like a dream, and I have new shoes to match it."

Julia glanced at the unwiped dishes in the drainer but didn't say anything. She wiped out the sink and counter, folded her towel-apron, and followed Julia into the bedroom.

Julia switched the bedroom light on, and opened the large closet door. She pulled out a covered dress, hung it up on the wall hook next to the closet, and opened a shoe box. A pair of sparkly heels which would most likely hurt her feet and be worn only once, were removed and placed under the dress. She continued to talk about the club activities as she removed the cover from the dress, hung it back on the hook and, and stood back to admire the sparkling ensemble.

"Of course, I was asked to be head of the planning committee this year, so I know the dinner will be wonderful. And…" Julia continued talking about the dinner and what would be served and the dancing and the two orchestras hired to play and the sunrise breakfast with real imported champagne, not just that sparkling wine, and the decorations which included beautiful fresh flowers flown in from Europe, and on and on, but June saw the price tag on the gown and held her breath. This gown would pay three months of their mortgage. Three months. And who knew what those shoes cost? She nodded her head and listened and tried to think of something to say.

"So, what do you think?"

"The gown and shoes are absolutely beautiful, Julia. You will be lovely, and I'm sure you'll have a wonderful time."

Julia nodded in agreement. As she re-covered the dress and

placed the shoes away, she thought to ask about June and Peter's plans. "Are you and Pete planning something special? What will you do to celebrate the new year?"

June smiled. "Certainly nothing like you have planned. A few of the neighbors get together at someone's house. We take turns, and this year we're going to the Murphy's house. All the kids will come and play games and watch television, and the adults will bring a dish to share. This year I'm trying a new casserole…a cheesy cheddar broccoli and macaroni casserole, and then I'm bringing my usual pineapple upside-down cake. Everyone seems to like it. At midnight, the kids make lots of noise, and we all go home. Nothing fancy, but we play cards and laugh, and it's a friendly time. Everyone will sleep in late the next day, and I'll have the ham and potatoes and a nice meal to start the new year. We'll just watch television and the kids will play games. Maybe some of their friends will come over. Both Peter and I have Thursday through Sunday off, so we're planning to catch up with some of the housework. We live a simple life, Julia. Nothing fancy. Nothing like yours."

Julia didn't say anything. Just then Daniel poked his head around the corner and said, "Dad says that Ed Sullivan is over and we should leave. It's still snowing, and he said we need to get going. Are we going home now?"

"Yes. Tell Dad I'm coming."

The two cousins walked out of the bedroom. Julia turned out the light, and they went into the hallway where everyone was getting on their boots and hats and coats.

"I'll go downstairs with you," Arnold said to Peter, and the two men left. Daniel and Deborah hugged their Aunt Julia and thanked her for the additional gifts they carried. They waited as their mother and aunt said their good-byes. Julia watched as they walked out of her glass-surrounded apartment. She waved until the door of the elevator closed, blocking them from her sight, whisking them to the ground floor. She closed the door and turned back to the empty, hushed apartment.

The snow drifted down onto the lake, and lights from the city could be seen glimmering through the sheerness, through muteness. The television was off. Nothing sounded, and the solitude created a semblance of loneliness and sadness. She thought about her lovely beaded gown hanging in the closet, the sparkly heels ready in their box, and she suddenly experienced a surge of anger although she was uncertain as to the reason. Walking over to the tall glass window, she looked out thinking she might be able to see June and Peter and their children driving to their home, but she could not observe anything in the swirl of snow. Julia stood, placing her hands on the cold transparency and, not meaning to, sighed. Turning towards the kitchen she decided to make herself another Harvey Wallbanger. Damn the sugar.

Chapter 21   Changing

June changed her mind about going to the town library.

It wasn't necessary.

She changed her mind about Julia's mischance.

She changed her mind about poisoning.

Poisoning was too risky.

So were stabbing, shooting, drowning, choking, and electrocuting.

She changed her mind about a car accident.

A car accident was out of the question.

It was too difficult to control.

The solution, to June's changed mind, was a regular accident.

The ultimate, ideal, perfect remedy.

She simply needed to wait.

Chapter 22   1975 Age 45

"No, Mama, you are not well enough to fly down there… Yes, I know she was your friend and sister-in-law, and I feel just as bad as you do. She was my aunt after all…I don't know…No, I'm not going…Yes, June got a flight and she leaves this afternoon. I hope so…she has never been on a plane before. No, a taxi… Peter and the kids are driving down tomorrow…I think two days, but they will be there in plenty of time…I guess so…Just one night…Not sure, but today is Monday and the plans are not set yet…Probably Thursday or Friday and most likely the funeral is Saturday…No, not for sure…I'll let you know…You need to listen to me. You aren't well and haven't felt good lately, and remember, you hated the plane trip two years ago when Uncle Henry died…Yes, it was lucky I was along because you were panicked, and I'm not sure what would have happened, but now it's two years later and Mama, you are older and not any healthier, and I'm not going…I told you…I can't… Arnie and I are leaving in a week for our month-long cruise, and I have lots to do this week…Well, packing and there are two committee luncheons I MUST attend, and Arnie and I have plans for dinner Friday night with an important client…Just sit down and stop crying…Mama… Mama, get Mrs. Sampson, I want to talk to her……………"

"Mrs. Sampson, please give Mama one of those pink pills from the doctor to calm her down. She is upset that she can't go to the funeral, and …What?...No, I can't go either…Well, that's the way it is…Has she eaten anything today?...Try and get her to eat a little something before you give her that pill. I am sure she needs to take it with food. Check the instructions…No, I can't get over there right now, but if she doesn't calm down, call Doctor Benson. I'll look up the number for you if you just hold on…Oh, you do have it…I need to do many things this week, but I'll try to get there later, in a few days. Maybe Thursday…Yes, that will be fine…OK…You can do that…Fine…Thanks, Mrs. Sampson… OK…I'll call later today and check in with you. Good-bye."

***

"Yes, this is Mrs. Wagner; may I speak to Mrs. Schroder? Yes…Hello, Cynthia, it's Julia Wagner…Fine, and you?...that's great…I'm calling to check on the number of replies for Wednesday's meeting…Ten? OK…Did Roberta Hamlin say anything about the flower arrangements for next month's dinner/dance?...Would you mind calling her and gently reminding her? I know she's busy, but she did say she would take care of it for me since I'm going to be gone for a

few weeks…Thanks so much…What time will you be at the Drake?…
Wonderful…No, I haven't heard from her about that. Maybe we'll find
out at the luncheon…Fine… I'll see you at the hotel…No, the usual
room, and I'll be there early like we planned…Yes, OK…Thanks, again,
Cynthia. Good-bye."

***

"Yes, hello Candace, this is Mrs. Wagner. Is Mr. Wagner
available?…Hello, Arnie. I hope I'm not disturbing you…I did call
Mama, and she thinks she needs to fly to Florida for the wake and
funeral, but that is absolutely not possible…You know how upset she
was when we flew down a couple years ago for Uncle Henry, and she is
just not well, and I don't think she could stand the trip, and this week is
just impossible for me, so there is no way to get there. I doubt the funeral
will be large anyway…No, I don't want to cancel the trip. We planned it
months ago, and both of us need a break, and I have already started the
packing…Mrs. Wilson is here now cleaning, and I told her not to make
any dinners this week unless you will be home tonight…You will? Then
I'll have her make it. Will a chicken dish be OK? I'll tell her to use up
what's in the freezer since we'll be gone all those weeks…Good…Yes,
June is leaving soon and Peter and the kids will drive down tomorrow…
No, I don't think so…I guess she'll stay in the apartment, and I suppose
she'll be there a while cleaning and packing and taking care of things…
She'll be fine. June is good at taking care of things…Alright, I'll
hold…………………………….."

"You're back…What were we talking about? Oh, yes, I wanted
to run something past you. When I know for certain about the wake
and the doings, we'll have a large flower arrangement sent down. Can
Candace do that? I'll get the information to her…Great…And Arnie,
I want to help out, so since I'm not going to be there, I want to get a
nice card and send it to June with a check. How much do you think?…
That much?…Well, I'll have Mrs. Wilson get an appropriate card and
you can write the check when you get home tonight. I'll get it mailed
by tomorrow…Yes, I have some meetings this week and need to get my
hair and nails done and pick up your clothes at the cleaner. No, wait,
I'll have them delivered. I don't have time to do that…Another call?
Well, go do your work and I'll see you tonight. About seven?…OK, see
you then…Bye."

***

"Hello, yes, this is Mrs. Wagner. My housekeeper dropped off my husband's clothes last week and they will be ready for tomorrow's pick-up. However, I'm going to need those delivered to the apartment…Yes, that is correct…No, the doorman will be able to accept them. I'll make sure he knows…That will be fine…Yes, do that…Great. Thank you."

***

"Hello. Mrs. Sampson? How is Mama?...Great, and did she eat something before you gave her a pill?...That's wonderful, she needs the sleep…Is that why you called?...Oh, well if there are only two left, is a refill available ?...Well, call the doctor's office, and get one, and if they need to speak to me, have them call. I'm going to be here for the next couple of hours, but I have a late lunch date with a friend at one, so do it before then…Yes, that will do…Thank you, Mrs. Sampson. I'm not sure what we'd do without you…I'm going to send Roy over tomorrow with our itinerary for the trip and the phone numbers and things you might need…Thanks…and I'll really try to get there on Thursday. Maybe Saturday after my hair appointment will be better, but I won't be able to stay long. I'll let you know for sure…Fine…OK…Bye, Mrs. Sampson."

***

"…and then, would you make sure the salad dressing is made? Thanks, Mrs. Wilson. I'm leaving now, but there is some cash on the counter for the sympathy card. Please make sure it is large and lovely and don't get one where the message is too gushy. Just a simple sympathy note. And get an expensive Hallmark card. This is my aunt, and I want it to be nice…I expect to be back around five or so…Yes, that will be fine…I'll see you Wednesday if I don't see you later…Great…Thanks again…Bye."

Chapter 23   Waiting

June was a patient person. Julia was irascible. June was solicitous. Julia was cantankerous. June did what Julia wanted her to do. She waited on her. She was obliging and placid and tolerant. She was willing to delay. To bide her time. Julia continued with her unpleasant, disagreeable attitude, moaning about her life and at least twice, regaled June with her order: "Just get it over with, June. Kill me. Really, this is an awful life. Why me? Why me?" and she sighed loudly. Twice. June did not respond.

While waiting for the right time, the time when her cousin would heal enough to have an additional regular accident, June, of necessity, gave up some of her own activities. She waited on Julia and therefore found it necessary to curtail the time she was absent from the townhouse they shared. She cut down on her walks around the lake. Sometimes she did not make it to the fitness class. The swimming class was discontinued. Talks and walks with Alice diminished, and when the local high school orchestra advertised an additional concert, Mrs. Crenshaw called to ask if she should save June a seat. She replied that she was sorry to miss the concert, but she would not attend this time. She could not. She stayed home with Julia. Just in case she was needed.

June completed tasks that Julia could have, should have, done. Flowers were sent to the house for Julia. "Write a note to these people, June. Make it a good one," and June wrote the thank-you notes, making sure they were good ones. Phone calls came for Julia who refused to talk to anyone. June answered the calls which her cousin dismissed with a wave of her hand. June was pleasant, even when telling little white lies ("So sorry; Julia is sleeping just now. Yes, I'll tell her you called, and thank you for thinking of her.") June did all these things and did not complain. She was waiting. She was patiently waiting.

Sometimes neighbors who had heard of the accident stopped by to check on Julia who instructed June to answer the door and "Get rid of them!"

"How is the PT going? Is your cousin improving? Is she able to hobble around yet? And aren't you wonderful to drive Julia there and wait for her all those times!" voiced Dr. Bennett after he stopped by for a friendly check on Julia. June informed him that her cousin was taking a nap although, in truth, she was sitting in her bedroom, the door partly closed, waiting for the doctor to leave.

"Julia is doing well. Her physical therapist said next week she should be able to cut down to twice a week. Thank you for coming, Dr. Bennett. I know Julia will be sad she missed you."

"Make sure she keeps up her at-home practice. That is extremely important, especially at our age. You are a good cousin to her. Have a pleasant day!" and the doctor left.

Physical therapy took up a great deal of June's time. The round-trip to the medical building took an hour, and June was nervous driving because she had to drive Julia's car. Her cousin refused to get into any car except her own because, she claimed, it was the only car she trusted. June had a back-seat driver, a literal back-seat driver. Julia sat in back insisting she was more comfortable there. Her instructions were yelled into the driver's ear. "Move into the next lane now, June. NOW! Honestly, you are a terrible driver. That's just what I need to have happen: be involved in a car accident with you driving! You need to be more careful!" In the front seat, June took some cleansing breaths and carefully moved to the next lane.

June always took a book with her when she waited for Julia. She knew there would be time to read because the sessions often extended well over the one hour scheduled. The physical therapist needed to encourage Julia to complete her exercises. "Mrs. Wagner, please do ten more. I know your ankle hurts, but this will improve it. No, we don't need to contact your doctor. Really, I *do* know what I'm doing." June overheard the comments and felt sorry for the therapist.

When therapy first started, Julia went Monday, Wednesday, and Friday, and she insisted upon June helping her dress on those days. June thought an ankle fracture shouldn't keep her cousin from pulling a dress on over her head, but apparently it did. On the days there was no therapy, Julia stayed in her nightgown and robe. As benefits an invalid. Breakfast was only tea and toast on PT days, but by the time the cousins returned, Julia was famished and wanted a healthy lunch which included dessert. Dinner was a salad, with the vegetables cut and sliced exactly as Julia required them. There was always something to be done. When the sessions were finally reduced to twice a week (Tuesday and Thursday), both June and the therapist were relieved. June could tell by the chest-heaving sigh the therapist gave as she walked Julia out to the car each time. It wasn't necessary, and other patients didn't receive this personal treatment, but Julia had insisted upon it. "I just need you nearby," she said to the therapist who walked with her, "I would hate to take your means of livelihood away should I fall and then I would need to sue. I would just feel so bad." The therapist walked next to her, opening the car's back door, and making sure Julia was secure as June slowly pulled out and traveled back to the Winchester Complex.

June waited. She waited for Julia. She waited for her to come to breakfast. She waited for her to complete her therapy sessions. She waited for her to eat her lavish lunch and her nightly salad so she could wash the dishes. She waited until Julia was healed. Because once she was safely walking with her cane ("I will probably need this cane for the rest of my life. I don't care what that therapist woman tells me. She doesn't know the pain I am in constantly!"), once June could determine exactly what sort of regular accident Julia would encounter, once she subdued her cousin, June's life would change for the better. And for that, she was willing to wait.

Cerumen Physical Therapy Center

*Where **CARE** is our primary goal!*

Check in upon entering

Remain in waiting area until called

No food or drink allowed

Children under 16 not allowed

Do not litter

No, we cannot change the TV station or watch your personal items

Your promptness is required.

You will be billed $50 if you miss your appointment and do not give us a 24-hour notice.

Approved: Dr. Henry Dropsy

Chapter 24   1980 Age 50

As Julia gazed into her compact mirror, turning her head to the left and then to the right, she smiled at herself. Then she looked once again at both sides before asking June, "Well, what do you think?"

June finished slicing the lemons which she put in a plate and set on the table so that Julia could create the tea she insisted on drinking ("Really, the best we found in England, and I won't, just won't drink the swill that's passed off for tea here in the States!" she explained to June.) She brought over a large tin of the special loose tea and the honey Julia insisted be kept for her when she visited. The water was boiling, and after June poured some into the cup, Julia made her tea and glanced at her watch noting the time she started the process. Exactly four minutes was needed. Not more. Never less.

"So, what do you think?" she repeated, presenting first one profile and then the other side to her cousin.

"Your nose looks fine, Julia. But I didn't really see anything wrong with it before, and still don't understand the reason for the surgery."

"A fiftieth birthday gift to myself! My nose needed correcting, and Doctor Bynion was highly recommended to me by three women at the Art League who had their work done by him. I was lucky to be able to get this done so early this year. I wanted a new nose before Deborah's wedding this summer, and I am really pleased with it. You should consider doing something before Deborah's wedding. You know, there is a new type of fat removal being done, but I'm unsure it is being done here in Chicago, and maybe it can't be done before the wedding anyway. Too bad. Just think how good you would look with some of that extra weight off," and Julia took a sip of her perfectly created four-minute seeped tea.

June looked at her. There was little sense in replying to the comments her cousin just made. It wasn't the first time Julia had commented on June's size, and it wouldn't be the last. June was learning to ignore the indelicate remarks, or perhaps she was simply getting used to them. She was determined not to argue and understood that Julia was probably still grieving. Aunt Maria had been buried at the beginning of the year, and June assumed that this current embrace of self-improvement by Julia was her attempt to deal with the death of her mother. Besides, there was so much work to be done for Deborah's wedding, and since

Julia had offered to help with the making of the favors, she dismissed the comments. Today, she actually needed her cousin's help.

"Julia, you look lovely, and whatever type of fat removal you think I might require, I'm not going to undergo any kind of surgery. Even if I could afford it, or have any time off work to recover, I don't see any reason to. I am perfectly fine; my dress fits, and it is the bride who should and will have all the attention anyway. I'm going to get the boxes so I can show you what we need to do," and June walked into the back bedroom, bringing out the two large boxes containing materials for the favors. As Julia finished her tea, June showed her how to fold the small cardboard boxes which would be filled with Jordan Almonds and sealed a week before the wedding.

"Why not just put the almonds inside now?" questioned Julia.

"Because we don't have them yet. We need to get these boxes ready. Filling them will be easy. This first part will take the most time, and I told Deborah that you would be here to help today. She is going to take the boxes over to the Maid of Honor's house the week before the wedding, and she and the two bridesmaids are going to fill them. Deborah wants everyone to have a task to do. She said that way friends and family will feel connected to the wedding in a meaningful way. I think it's that teacher training stuff that made her think of this."

"Humph," commented Julia as she pushed the empty tea cup away, "and what meaningful connection does her brother have in the creation of this wedding?"

June laughed. "Now, Julia, leave Daniel alone. He is the head usher and has agreed to both wear a tuxedo and get a haircut, and I am happy with that. So is Deborah. At least the wedding will be held before he goes back to college in the fall, so I am sure he will be here. He has his own ideas about life, and I have learned to let him be. Don't hold grudges because of the past."

"Oh, please, you know me. I don't do that. I have forgiven him for crashing and destroying my new car when he was sixteen. My fault. I should never have allowed him to drive it," and Julia thought back to that time and sighed. "I'll be anxious to see him cleaned up and dressed up, and looking decent for a change. Where are the two of them anyway? I thought I'd see Debbie today. It's a Saturday, and school is almost out for the summer, so I'm sure she's not grading papers."

"Daniel's working, and Deborah and her father went to the mall to look at tuxedos. They were meeting Robert and his groomsmen there, and Deborah wanted a say-so in the kind of outfits they would wear. She is headstrong and lucky that Robert doesn't mind. I really like her fiancé. I think it's a good match."

"Remember my wedding?" and Julia stopped folding the box to stare into space. "It was lovely. So many people, and such a great time. Mama and I worked on it for most of a year. I think there were almost three hundred people there. The orchestra was so good, and the food! Of course, this wedding won't be as elaborate, but I am sure it will be fine. There weren't any favors that had to be made for mine, but then this seems to be something new. Almonds. Too hard for the teeth. At least I've never liked them. I know those Jordan ones will have a candy coating. That will help the awful taste. Arnie and I had those matchboxes and napkins engraved with our names. They were done in silver, or were they gold? Anyway, everyone said they were lovely and so elegant. Do you remember?"

"Yes, I remember."

"Of course, your wedding was so simple. It was nothing like mine. No favors or matchboxes or anything like that. A plain wedding, if I remember. Too bad you and Peter couldn't have a real honeymoon like the one Arnie and I had."

"Yes, Julia, a plain wedding which was perfect for Peter and me. There wasn't much money, and Mom and Dad gave us what they could, and we put it away for a down payment on this house. We are plain people, Julia. Your side has the money."

Julia looked at June, her newly created upturned nose tipped just so. She was surprised at the tone in June's voice. A tone of regret? Jealously? Resentment? Bitterness? Not like June at all. A diminutive feeling of satisfaction entered Julia's essence. Perhaps she should continue this conversation.

"I can't help it that my family was well-off, June. Daddy just knew how to make money and Mama knew how to spend it on the nicest things. And remember, Arnie's family was already wealthy, so there's that. You have a perfectly nice small house here, and soon it will be just the two of you. Unless Danny decides to live here after college. What is his degree going to be in?"

"Daniel is studying something called technology and computer science. Don't ask me what that means. I'm not sure, but he says it's going to be important in the future. I hope he's right. I tried to talk him into being a teacher like his sister, but he said he didn't have the patience for it. He still has another year, and I'm not sure what his plans are. He's welcome to stay here with us, but I doubt that he would want to. Wait, Julia, you folded that one incorrectly. Did you do them all that way?"

Julia looked at the box in her hand and shrugged. "I did what you showed me. Anyway, this is the last one I can do. It's getting late, and I need to go. I need to get ready. Arnie and I are meeting friends for dinner tonight. Do you have any plans for later?"

"Not really. Peter will probably find something to watch on television, and I want to finish the library book I'm reading which is due next week."

Pushing the chair back, Julia got up to stretch and then got out her compact once again. She looked at her nose and turned her head to see the other side. "Can't wait for Cynthia to see me tonight. I haven't seen her because she and her husband have been on a trip, and now that my nose is healed, she is sure to be jealous. Her nose is just a bit crooked, and she is thinking about getting something done to it. She should. It isn't getting better with age. Well, thanks for the tea, and tell Debbie I helped as much as I could. I guess the next time I see you will be at the wedding. I have the loveliest dress for it!"

June stood up and walked her cousin out to the front. She waved as the red convertible Corvette took off and returned to the kitchen where she placed the tea cup and the plates into the sink, put away the honey and imported tin of tea, and looked at the dozen boxes Julia had folded. When she realized they were all folded incorrectly, she sighed and murmured a gentle oath under her breath. Glancing at the clock, she decided that tonight, instead of reading her book, she would need to unfold and then refold Julia's boxes. Typical. June placed the materials into the larger boxes, moved them to the side and went to the sink where after she washed the dishes, she would begin to make the Saturday night supper.

Chapter 25   #5 Mrs. Sampson

I'm not much of a Bible reader, but Theresa is fond of repeating something from one of the books; something about the sun rising and setting and always going back to the same place. She told me that it means life is a circle, and I guess that has some truth to it. Just like when we were young, Theresa and I are back living together. Back in our circle of two.

I don't mind it. We are getting used to each other again just like she got used to being a widow. Her husband, John, died a few years back, and her youngest daughter married, moved out, and is living with her husband and new baby (Theresa now has five grandchildren.) so my sister was by herself for a while. Then when Mrs. Reynolds died, and I knew I would need to leave that red-bricked house and find my own place, she asked if I'd like to live with her again, just like when we were girls. I did because there was not much choice for me, and after all, we are family. Even if she's Mrs. Tanner and I still keep the name of Eliza Sampson. I have been called that for so long I pretty much forgot I created the name for myself. Mrs. Sampson. That's who I am.

I do miss Mrs. Reynolds at times. Maybe not so much her as the large red-bricked house I cleaned for so many years and thought of as mine. I miss Roy, the driver, and his wife who became my friends. He retired, and they moved down to some place in southern Illinois where two of their children live with their families. I have their address, and we send Christmas cards back and forth, and they always ask me to come for a visit. I tell them maybe next year. But I know I'll never visit them. I think they know it too.

Mrs. Reynolds thought I was five years older than she was, and in her clearer moments, would comment about how young I seemed. Of course, I lied about that and was much younger in age than her, but I did that to get the job. Not sorry about my lying. Sometimes it's necessary to do that to get ahead. Just need to stick to it and not forget what you said. Keep it simple. Another thing I don't regret is the small things I took from the many curio cabinets in the house. She was always getting gifts, and so many were expensive. And useless. I could see that. For years, I cleaned them and found places for them in the cabinets, rearranging them so they could all be seen. There were so many that it was never noticed when I took a few to the pawn shop. I always got a good price for them. I put that money with the other money I saved. I knew that one day I would not be working and would need to support myself. That's another reason why Theresa and I live together. Cheaper.

Mrs. Reynolds grew a bit forgetful as the years passed. Especially once her brother Henry died and she went to Florida for the funeral. Julia went with her, and I guess the trip was awful. It was the first time Mrs. Reynolds was on a plane, and she didn't take to the ride. On their way home, Julia got some kind of pills to give her and I guess she slept most of the way. When Henry's wife, Rose, died and she wasn't able to go to that funeral, she sat and cried and begged Julia to take her. Julia was planning a big vacation trip and wouldn't go, but I felt bad for Mrs. Reynolds. She kept saying to me that they were all gone, and she didn't care to be left by herself. She lost interest in her clubs and such, but to be fair, most of those clubwomen were either sick or moved to somewhere like Florida or Arizona. Many of the ones who stayed here died, and I accompanied her as Roy drove us to the funerals. Mrs. Reynolds would cry all the way there and back, even when it was one of the women she didn't particularly like.

Her death wasn't so easy either. I took care of her as she stayed up in her big bedroom. When there were good days, she sat up in the big easy chair in the corner and watched the television Arnold had put in for her years earlier. The last couple of months she was in the house, she never even went downstairs. I would climb the stairs many times a day to bring her tea and meals, but she rarely finished anything I made for her. Honestly, I don't know exactly what was wrong with her. The doctor gave her lots of pills which I had to make sure she took, and somedays those pills and the tea were the only things that entered her stomach. They didn't always stay there. She was skin and bones.

When she got so sick and had to be moved to the hospital, I would sit there with her for hours, talking to her when she was awake, listening to her stories told over and over again, and holding her hand. She would ask if Julia was home from school yet, and did June come with her, and what was I making for the important dinner Mr. Reynolds needed to host, and where was Princess, and all such past remembrances. The last few days, I didn't leave her side. June came in to see her and stayed for a while, but Julia was away on one of her trips. At the end, when Mrs. Reynolds got so bad, I told June to get in touch with her cousin and tell her she needed to get home right away. Julia was on her way when her mother died. I sat holding her hand and I cried, in part, for myself. When Julia did get into the room and saw her mother laying there, me stroking her cold hand, she fell into Arnold's arms, and I went over to her and comforted her as she sobbed so hard that Arnold asked for a doctor to tend to his wife. A terrible time.

I was asked to stay in the house for some months until the house and everything in it could be packed up and sold, and I was glad to. Julia still paid me for those months although the pay envelope came just twice a month and not three or four times like Mrs. Reynolds, in her forgetfulness, would do. I helped to pack and label all the things in the house. There was more than I realized, and I made many trips to the pawn shop with gifts and treasures and even jewelry that had never been opened or worn. When Julia came over some days to help, she would look at some of the things and shake her head. "What a waste. Mama never even wore these (or displayed this, or opened this)," she would say, and then tell me that I could have it if I wanted it. So, some of the things I took to the shop were honest gifts.

It was during this time Theresa and I planned our living together. Julia told me I could have any furniture I wanted, and there were a few things I did take. Of course, the new television set was one, and there was a nice chair or two and a sofa that would replace the old furniture that Theresa's family had lived through. Then the dining room table and chairs came too, as Theresa's old broken down one was removed. My bedroom set had a new one-year old mattress, and that went along with the dresser and chest and a few lamps. The old washing machine at Theresa's house needed replacing so I took the one from the Reynolds' house, and their dryer was a bonus since my sister didn't have one. I guess I basically replaced all Theresa's old stuff with the expensive things from the Reynolds' house. Julia didn't care. She was thoughtful and hired movers to get everything there. After about four months, the house was emptied, the furniture gone, the doo-dads sold or given away. I was in the house with Theresa, and the large red-bricked two-story house was sold to a family who had three children. I wished them luck.

Julia was always kind to me. Of course, I wasn't her mother and didn't argue with her about what she should do, and there weren't loud disagreements between us. I had seen the girl grow up. Had changed her diapers as a baby, fed her after school treats, helped her with the wedding and settled her in that new apartment. I watched over her with her sadness and wiped up the blood from the last baby she lost. I knew her. And I didn't. I guess that people do change, and while Julia was always good to me and mostly listened, I saw a difference in her as she aged. She became mean. Not just to that dog, but to her mother and her husband, Arnie and her cousin, June. I overheard her on the telephone to others. She repeated things she shouldn't have and hurt feelings, and I heard her tell a lie or two. Maybe it was due to the fact she was a spoiled child. She was. Single children are often like that, but not all. I saw June, and she was not spoiled. Maybe the loss of her babies twisted Julia in a way I couldn't understand. As she aged, she turned vain. She had a perfectly fine nose, but complained about it and went through that surgery right after her mother's death. Frankly I couldn't tell the difference. Arnold spoiled her too, and I suspected there were times, one or two although I was never positive about it, that she didn't stick to her marriage vows. Maybe she felt guilty about these times. I don't really know. How much can we see into the hearts of others?

Julia never forgets me. Every holiday there is a gift for me. She regularly visits me, and when she comes, she always brings a present for me and something for Theresa too. Around the first of each month, there is a note in the mail, in Julia's bad penmanship, letting me know that she's thinking of me. A check is included. It isn't enough to cover all the household bills, but it's enough to cover most of them, and Theresa and I don't have many. I took some of my pension savings, and when I moved in with Theresa, I paid off the remainder of her mortgage. My gift to her.

Theresa and I enjoy living together. We talk about our past and speak of our mother and wonder about our father. We became friends with two or three other old women on the street, and every couple of weeks, we all get together at someone's home and each of us brings a dish to share, and we talk and laugh and play cards and share the bottle of whiskey I always bring. At least every month, one of Theresa's children has us over for a dinner, and we spend the holidays together with her children and grandchildren, and I hardly miss not having any. Her children are mine too.

Times are good, and I enjoy being with my sister again. Periodically I look at the society pages in the newspaper and see a picture of Julia and Arnold as they dance at some party, or Julia and some of the women she has as friends, sitting around a table eating a luncheon at a big downtown hotel and grinning for the camera. There are often mentions of Arnold in the business section, and more than once, they were photographed with a large group, standing with the mayor and some of the aldermen at an important function. I always look closely at these pictures, and examine Julia when she comes to visit. I pay particular attention to her eyes. Her nose is perfect, and her smile large, and her clothes and hair excellent, but I never see any happiness in her eyes. Not in the photographs. Not in person. And when she leaves from the visits, I make sure to hug her tight; to try and squeeze into her some of the happiness I have found in coming back to where my sun is setting and where I am completing my own circle.

Ecclesiastes 1:5-7

The sun also ariseth, and the sun goeth down, and
hasteth to his place where he arose.

The wind goeth toward the south, and turneth
about unto the north; it whirleth about continually,
and the wind returneth again according to his
circuits.

All the rivers run into the sea; yet the sea *is* not full;
unto the place from whence the rivers come, thither
they return again.

Chapter 26   Devising

"Mrs. Wagner, try the stairs without the cane. You won't fall. Your ankle is much stronger, and stair-walking will help it. We have practiced this, and you can do it," and the therapist gave a quick side glance to the wall clock to determine how much longer the current session needed to continue.

Julia should have been done with her physical therapy weeks ago, but she insisted her doctor approve additional sessions. She claimed she still needed her cane, and while the stairs she was forced to maneuver presented a problem, she was, according to the therapist, doing well and did not need to use it. The therapist explained to her that now, walking without the cane was the best activity for her. Walking up and down stairs was a useful functional exercise, and she should do it daily. It would help her ankle and her knees and her general health. Julia nodded her head and as June drove her home, she complained: "That woman does not know what she is talking about. She should see how I struggle!"

June said nothing. While Julia had been given the go-ahead to begin driving again, she continued to insist June chauffeur her. However, she now sat in the front passenger seat. This made it easier to correct the driver. And Julia did.

Life for June continued to be distressing and grim. Julia continued her complaints about the coffee smell, her insistence on being waited upon, her contention that she was impaired for the rest of her life. She seemed to manage perfectly well without a cane while at home, but she took it everywhere else. Not because she needed it. It was a source of sympathy and commiseration, and Julia relished explaining about her "…unfortunate, near fatal accident" in front of Mr. Simmons' house to anyone they met during the walks she and June took.

June continued to count on a regular accident happening to Julia. At night, as she lay in bed waiting for sleep, she considered what life would be like without her cousin. She thought about making her coffee and being able to enjoy it without complaints about the smell, about having a second cup of the beverage, about reconnecting with friends and neighbors and resuming activities she gave up, about having some plants or flowers in the house, about living in her own little place. It was a dream to which she fell asleep. And early in the morning, just as the sun was beginning to shine and there was no sound coming from the other occupied bedroom, she went into the kitchen to brew and enjoy her only cup of coffee, to smell its aroma, and for a brief while, be satisfied with life. But a plan needed to be devised. June could not have her activities and coffee aroma and flowers unless she came up with a strategy.

June encouraged Julia to exercise her ankle, so the two cousins went for daily walks. They didn't walk around the path or travel too far from their townhouse at first. Only to the end of their street and back. Then across the street. Then down two streets. Finally, they were walking as far as the Winchester Complex's common building. One day, June suggested they go inside the building and walk around the first floor. Once they entered, Julia decided she needed to rest and took one of the chairs in the front by the large window. As she sat there, resident tenants walked by and greeted her. Some noticed her cane which she placed directly in front of her, and they asked about it. Julia repeated the sad story of her fall. She was happiest when bemoaning her fate.

It was during one of these sessions a plan was formulated. Julia was explaining to a woman, a new tenant in the complex, about her near fatal accident while June took the time to walk up the stairs to the Winchester Complex's library to look for a book. She looked through the stack of mystery novels, found one she hadn't read, and returned to the top of the stairs. She stood there holding the novel and looked down. She watched as Julia continue her lengthy explanation to the other woman, and as she looked down the flight of stairs, to the bottom, she remembered.

June came down the stairs. Carefully. She walked over to her cousin and spoke. "Julia, why don't you walk up and down the flight of stairs over there. Your therapist always suggests you do that; that it will help you heal. Come on. I'll go up behind you this first time. Then we'll go home."

To her surprise, Julia agreed, and, using her cane, she went to the bottom of the stairs and began, slowly, to climb them. She got to the top and turned to June. "That wasn't so bad. I did a great job, don't you think?"

June nodded. "Yes, you did. Be careful going down."

Julia was careful. When they got to the bottom, June said, "That was good practice for you. You did a fine job. Let's go home now. We can do this each time we take a walk, and soon you'll be good as new."

She held the front door open for her cousin. They walked outside and slowly began the short trek home. As they crossed the first street, Julia stopped for a moment. She looked down at her feet and then up at her cousin. "I'm going to need to soak my ankle when we get home. You can bring the bucket with Epsom salts to the front room and set it up there. I'll watch television as it soaks. And then you can rub it with that cream. And you can make me a cup of tea. Also, I want some toast. I'm hungry and I need to rest."

"Of course you do," said June.

Winchester Senior Complex Library

Fiction Section

Take a Book

Leave a Book

Share with your friends

Chapter 27   1985 Age 55

"How have you been coping since our last meeting, June?"

"I've been better, Doctor Spanner. I have tried the cleansing breaths you told me to take when the thoughts about Peter overwhelm me, and that has helped. I even told Julia about them because I don't think she has dealt with her mother's death very well. Of course, she hasn't listened, but I am doing better."

"Death is difficult, and the passing of one's spouse is particularly hard. We all have our own methods of coping, and you have made the first step in coming to see a therapist. And your family? How are your children doing?"

"They seem to be OK. Of course, they are adults and working, and busy with their lives. Deborah is teaching, and Daniel just started a new job and is excited about it. I admit I dread the thought of this year's holidays without Peter although Julia said her husband, Arnold, can stand in for him if needed. I'm unsure what she means and somehow that doesn't seem right, but Julia tries her best, I suppose. Anyway, the kids and I are in touch often, and I see them for dinners and such."

"So, you are getting better, and the children are too. That's good. How long has it been since Peter's death? One year?"

"Almost. One year next month. I was thinking about having the children over on that anniversary day. I thought we could have a nice dinner with Peter's favorite foods, and look at the family album and remember the good times, but perhaps that's not a good idea. Julia told me it sounds morbid, but then she has such strong opinions about everything. What do you think, Doctor Spanner?"

"I think you should run that idea past your children and see what they think. They might surprise you. It sounds like a healthy thing to do. Many cultures mark a year's anniversary doing similar things. Remember, we discussed *adjusting* and *readjusting*, and your plan sounds like both an adjustment to one situation and a readjustment to create another situation. Talk to your family and see what they think and want to do."

"I will. I'll also mention it again to Julia. Maybe she'll change her mind and show up. She said that the plan sounded so dreadful she didn't think she would come if I did that."

Doctor Spanner looked at June, jotted something in his notebook and changed his position in his chair. They were quiet for a few seconds, and then he spoke.

"You seem to be much better, and I'm pleased you have taken some suggestions and used them. But I'd like to mention something else; something not about Peter or how to deal with this adjustment in your life. We have only talked for about ten minutes and you have mentioned your cousin five times. I looked at my notes for the last time when you were here, and you mentioned Julia's name at least ten times, and the time before that, another nine times. I think we should talk about Julia. She's on your mind, and I wonder if there is more than one reason you wanted to talk to someone. When you completed your questionnaire, you wrote about wanting to talk about your grieving and get help dealing with your husband's passing. I know that is true, but after the first session we had, Julia's name has come up more often than has Peter's name. Is there another reason you are here? Is there something else we can discuss? Think about it for a minute."

June sat still. She did think. Peter's death from a heart attack a year ago was unforeseen and unanticipated. It was an awful time and she continued having difficulties accepting it. What did Julia have to do with it? She sighed and looked at Doctor Spanner.

"I didn't realize I was mentioning Julia so often. We are cousins, but were brought up almost like sisters. My father and her mother were siblings; we went to the same schools and stood up to each other's wedding. Julia has always had strong opinions, and sometimes they have really irritated me. In fact, at times, her comments are even cruel. She thinks she knows what's good for everyone just because her family has always had MONEY, and she thinks THAT gives her a RIGHT to be the BE All AND END ALL, AND SHE HAS HARDLY BEEN A HELP TO ME DURING THIS PAST YEAR AND NOW SHE IS IN EUROPE AGAIN FOR A MONTH-LONG VACATION AND…" June stopped suddenly when she noted she was yelling. The two of them sat quietly as that realization sunk in.

"I'm sorry," she said to the doctor, "I didn't mean to raise my voice. I'm not angry at you."

"I know that, June. But you are angry, and obviously it's at Julia. Let me ask some questions, and don't worry if you get loud. I'm just trying to understand. Where is Julia now? You said she's in Europe?"

"Yes. She and her husband left a week or so ago. They travel there almost every year. That's where they went on their honeymoon, and Julia loved it."

"They travel because they have money and can afford to. Correct?"

"I guess. I also think it's Julia's way of showing off. She always comes back with a new wardrobe and jewelry and invites me over to see it all."

"Do you think you are jealous?"

"Maybe somewhat. Peter and I had struggles, but then most of our friends and neighbors did also. Julia and I do not run in the same social circles. I went back to work part-time when the kids were in school, and we saved to be able to add another bedroom on the house so Deborah and Daniel didn't have to share. We bought used cars and tried to keep up with repairs on them while EVERY YEAR, JULIA HAS A NEW ONE, AN EXPENSIVE ONE…sorry, I'm yelling again."

"Don't worry about it. So, Julia has new things and expensive things and travels and seems to have a great life, right?"

"That's about it. I don't really care except she seems to lord it over me and thinks her money and jewels and traveling gives her a right to tell me what to do and how to do it. She has never worked except for a couple years when her father gave her a job in his office. That's where she met Arnold, her husband."

"What kind of a person is Arnold? Do you get along with him?"

"Arnold is a decent man. He puts up with Julia and spoils her just like her father did. He and Peter always got along and enjoyed being together. I don't have any gripes about Arnold. He's a good person. Too good because if he knew about…" and here June stopped. She didn't know anything for certain and feared she said too much.

Doctor Spanner looked up at June. He waited for her to finish her thought.

"Well, I don't know for sure. Julia hasn't been completely faithful to her husband. At least, that's what I suspect. And her mother, Aunt Maria, thought so too. I know they had more than one argument about it. I don't have any proof, and the only time it came up, I let Julia know what I thought. And I thought she was wrong. We never discussed it again. At least I never brought it up, unlike Julia who raises the same issues with me again and again."

"Such as?"

"She harps about me losing weight. She tells me to stop drinking coffee because TEA is so much healthier. She brings up the fact that when he was sixteen, my son, Daniel, drove her car and wrecked it, even though she gave him the keys and ENCOURAGED HIM TO DRIVE IT EVEN WHEN HE SAID HE WAS NOT SURE HE SHOULD... sorry. Julia tells me how I should dress, what I should do with my free time, that I should GET OVER PETER BECAUSE IT'S A DONE DEAL! Sorry. She even used those words."

Doctor Spanner nodded his head.

"You do have some issues with Julia, and maybe we can work on those. She is gone for a few weeks, and you won't need to deal with her, and perhaps together, we can come up with some techniques to use when she does return. Should we talk about her next time? Is there more you want to say about this relationship?"

"I guess that would be a good thing to do. Sometimes I get so angry I could just kill her, and then I feel really guilty even thinking that. I mean, we have had some good times too. Right now, except for my children, she is the closest family I have. I don't see us parting ways. On the other hand, I don't see us becoming closer. Yes, I guess I need to deal with my feelings about her."

"Good. Then we have a path to take for the next few sessions. I do have some homework for you. Come in next week and tell me about two memories concerning Julia. One should be a happy one and the other an unhappy one. Think about how you responded to each, and we'll talk about them. Is that acceptable?"

"It is, Doctor. I only hope I can narrow the unhappy instances down," and June let out a small giggle.

"I'm sure you will be able to," replied Doctor Spanner as he wrote furiously on his pad of paper.

Chapter 28   Resolving

If it hadn't been for the coffee carafe calamity, June may have changed her mind. If she thought it had truly been a mistake, an *accident*, a regular accident, she may very well have doubted her entire approach, reassessed her scheme, devised a different outcome, de-resolved her resolve. She was standing at the edge of the kitchen when it happened, and she knew it was no mischance, not a mishap, never a misfortune. Julia had broken it on purpose.

That day, June, as usual, readied her early morning coffee. She pulled out her old coffee maker and carafe, measuring coffee and water. But this morning, perhaps because she wanted to, she measured additional coffee and water for additional cups of the hot and tasty beverage. This morning she would drink more than one cup and was determined to ignore the comments which were sure to arise when Julia came in for her tea and breakfast. She arranged the coffee maker at the center of the counter, away from the new, still-in-the-box-never-opened-one-cup-at-a-time coffee maker which lingered in the opposite corner. The one that used the individual coffee capsules June had priced and deemed too expensive to purchase. It was there, dwelling alone, almost forgotten, never mentioned. The old coffee maker continued to render steadfast service, and June continued to use it. When Julia came into the kitchen and sat down at her place in front of the Manuka honey from New Zealand and the expensive imported Harrington tea and the thinly sliced fresh lemons, June was also seated at the table sipping her second cup of coffee, the aroma from the stalwart coffee maker and the carafe which contained supplemental brewed beverage filling the air in the kitchen and assailing Julia's nose like the poop from Mrs. Crenshaw's dog which once accosted it.

She sat down and crossed her arms and stared at June. She sat like that for a full minute before heaving a sigh and beginning the creation of her cup of tea. Nothing was said. No *good mornings* were exchanged. June sipped her coffee and paged though her current book, and Julia timed her brewing. She mixed just the exact amount of honey into the cup, placed a fresh lemon slice on top of the tawny tea, took a sip and created a noise which sounded like, "Brahnk!" She put the teacup down and looked at June who, with her periphery vision, could see Julia staring at her. She knew she was expected to ask what the matter was, but, this morning, emboldened by her second cup of coffee, June did not feel she wanted to capitulate to her cousin and steadfastly ignored her. At the second and louder, "Brahnk!", June gave in and looked up. "What's the problem, Julia?" she asked, marking her place in her book with her bookmark.

Julia pushed her cup away and sniffed. Then she squinched up her face as she explained, "The coffee is the problem. It stinks, and the smell has spoiled my tea. Why are you continuing to drink it? Aren't you usually finished with that vileness by now? Really, this is irritating!"

Something in June splintered. Perhaps it was the additional caffeine flowing through her system, but she stared back at Julia and slowly nodded her head. She sat up straight in her chair and took a deep breath. No cleansing breath this. It was the type of breath a bull might take as it views the waving cape which has annoyed it for the final time, dispensing with whatever slight patience it may have possessed, patience disappearing like the dust beneath the ground it paws.

"For years, Julia, I have gotten up early to make and drink my coffee so that the smell won't bother you. For years. I then wash everything up and make sure nothing remains to irritate your delicate nose. Today, I felt like another cup. I have a right to drink it here. In this kitchen we share. As I make YOUR breakfast every morning. I have a RIGHT to it, Julia!"

June stood up. She grabbed her coffee cup and guzzled the rest of it. Then she walked over to the carafe and poured more coffee into her cup, added cream, and sat down at the table. This was her THIRD cup. She didn't really want it but was making a point. She took a gulp of the coffee, plonked the cup on the table, and opened her book. As she found her page, she said without looking up, "Get your own breakfast today," and continued to read.

Julia sat still with her mouth agape. She was shocked. There was something exceedingly wrong with June. When she realized she was being ignored, Julia pushed herself away from the table and stood up. She removed the honey and the lemons and placed them on the counter. She cleaned up the tea and the spoon and the cup, dumping the now tepid liquid into the sink and put the cup and spoon and plate there. She did not do these tasks quietly, but made a fair amount of noise. Then she walked to the kitchen entry way where she turned to look at her cousin and to speak. But June was sipping her coffee and reading, and since she wasn't sure what to say, Julia simply walked into her bedroom.

June did not look up. Her heart was beating rapidly, and she couldn't concentrate on her book which she had only pretended to read. She looked at her coffee cup, and deciding she didn't want anymore, emptied it, settling the container into the sink. Next to Julia's tea cup. She decided to go to her room and ready herself for her fitness class. She would come back later and clean up.

Fifteen minutes later, June left for the class. Julia's bedroom door was still shut, and she paused before it. *Later,* she thought, *when I return, we can talk. She'll be calm then. So will I.* June began her walk to class and saw Alice standing on her front walk, waiting for her. Alice had her rolled-up yoga mat under her arm, and when June saw it, she remembered.

"I forgot we were to bring the mats today,' she said to Alice, "Go on ahead. I'll go back to get mine. See you in class," and June turned back to the house.

She opened the front door, walked through the hallway, and saw Julia's bedroom door was opened. June went into her own room, grabbed her mat, and hearing kitchen noises, decided to peek in and tell Julia that when she returned, they would talk about what had happened earlier.

Julia had washed the cups and spoons which were placed on the counter drainer and was at the sink holding the coffee carafe. A small amount of cold liquid remained in it, and she dumped it out. Holding the glass container over the stainless-steel sink, she stepped back a bit and opened her hand. The glass carafe fell to the emptied sink and shattered at the same moment June yelled "Stop!"

Julia looked at her cousin. It was June's mouth which was now agape. Horror filled the room as the women stared at each other. For what seemed like hours, there was a silence, and the only thing which could be heard was the catching of breaths and the gasping for air. To describe what took place afterwards would be impossible.

Yelling. Crying. Accusing. Excuses. Anger. Hostility. Resentment. Wrathfulness. Infuriation. Years and years of it all. And when the silence was heard again; when the excuses and apologies, insincere perhaps, were made; when an unsteady truce was obtained, June heard the refrain again. The rhythm grew constant and there were no word substitutions. Even days later, when she came into the kitchen and a large box, a new version of the old coffee maker with a sparkling brand-new glass carafe was on the table, she could not tamp down the litany. Her prefrontal cortex and hippocampus were working overtime, and with each step she took, with every outward breath, with the sighs escaping from the back of her throat, it was fixed; it was unvarying; it was undeviating, it was resolved: *Kill cousin Julia; Kill cousin Julia; Kill cousin Julia.*

Winchester Senior Complex

Senior Shape-Up

Reminder!

9:30-10:15

Monday, Wednesday, Friday

Bring a YOGA MAT for Wednesday classes

**Yoga Mats available for purchase at

front desk in Common Building**

$10

Chapter 29   1990 Age 60

Amy, June's two-year old granddaughter threw herself into her grandmother's arms crying, "No nap! No nap!" and June smiled at her daughter as she pulled Amy away.

"Come on, Amy. I'll rock you and read a book and then you can rest in Mommy's old bed. Won't that be fun?" Deborah held onto her daughter and moved slowly because her pregnant belly was in the way. They went into the bedroom that used to be Deborah's and Julia looked at June.

"How will she handle two of them? I hope the new baby is a boy. I think they're easier to deal with." And she took a sip of her iced tea.

June got up and refilled her ice water. She would have preferred coffee, but didn't want to hear Julia complain about the smell, so in her own house, in her own kitchen, she allowed her cousin to dictate what she drank. She was choosing her battles. Still following the advice from Doctor Spanner. Besides, there was tension in the air. June and Julia had an unpleasant and hurtful argument and hadn't spoken to or seen each other in almost two months until June broke down and called Julia, inviting her and Arnie over for a July cookout. Deborah and Daniel, their spouses and families would be visiting, and June thought a houseful of friendly, familiar relatives might ease the continuation of persistent agitation She specified the third of July because she assumed Julia and Arnie would be busy on the Fourth of July because they usually were. Julia said they would be happy to come over and see the family. Truce.

"Not so sure boys are easier. They have their own issues. But I know the trip here was a long one, and Deborah wants Amy to get some sleep. Otherwise, she'll be crabby for the fireworks tonight, and Deborah said that Amy has talked about little else since seeing some a few weeks ago. I wouldn't be surprised if Deborah lays down for a nap too."

Julia glanced at her new watch. Her new gold and diamond Piaget watch Arnold gave her for her sixtieth birthday. She stared at it and moved it around her wrist until June noticed and commented.

"Lovely watch, Julia," and then, having followed Doctor Spanner's instructions again to comment briefly and move on, she looked out the kitchen window hoping the car she heard was Daniel and his wife, Nancy, driving up. It was not.

"Yes, it is lovely. Arnie got me something very special for my birthday, and this is it," and Julia glanced at her cousin to see if she understood the veiled reference to the sixtieth birthday which June had purposely ignored. Not even a card had been sent. June continued to stare out the kitchen window, craning her neck to look down the street.

"Why are you looking out the window?"

"I thought Daniel and Nancy were driving up. It's almost eleven, and I was sure they would be here by now. There must be lots of holiday traffic and it's holding them up. Maybe they got a late start. I should see how Arnold and Robert are doing with the grill. Hopefully they got it set up and are ready to start, but I want to tell them to wait until Daniel and Nancy get here. Everything else is ready for lunch. Be right back," and June went to instruct the two men in the backyard.

When she returned, Julia was bent over looking in the refrigerator, moving things around and opening the covers of the dishes, peeking in to see what there was.

"They are fine. Just sitting outside, drinking a beer, and watching the coals get hot. Once everyone is here, the burgers and hot dogs can go on the grill. What are you looking for? Pull out that top dish. It has different cheeses and some olives, and I have some focaccia bread to put with it. I'll take a plate out for the guys, and we can snack in here. It's getting warm outside. I guess Deborah is sleeping with Amy. I don't hear her reading anymore."

The plate was readied and delivered to the backyard, and June came in to sit again at the kitchen table where she took a slice of the bread and some cheese. The kitchen fan blew across the table riffling the stack of red, white, and blue paper napkins, causing then to lift and move until June plopped some forks on the top one. She sat back, sipped her water, and looked at Julia who was placing one olive into her mouth. Then she wiped her mouth and sipped at her iced tea.

"This is good bread, Julia. Would you like some butter for a piece? There's also some of the Havarti cheese you like."

Julia shook her head. "No, I'll wait until lunch to eat something. Don't want to snack much today. Arnie and I have two important parties to attend tomorrow, and there will be food there too," and she glanced at her new watch again.

June said nothing. She finished her food. She was learning to not nag Julia who, according to Doctor Spanner, looked for what he called "inciting comments": ways to engage June in an argument. Laughter drifted in from the backyard, and the cousins sat quietly. Both making decisions about what conversation should be explored. Both coming to the same conclusion about not bringing up the past two months of uneasy reticence. Both hoping the other one would remain dumb about the previous disagreement. Both mulling over what had happened between them.

***

They had gone to lunch. Julia gave a rare invitation, asking June to be her lunch guest at her current favorite downtown club, after which they planned to do some shopping. June drove her car to the area, parked it at a public lot two blocks away, and walked to the club to wait for Julia who was, as usual, fashionably late. She waited outside the building until she saw Julia drive up in her new car (a red convertible), and the club's parking valet hurried out to greet her ("Hello, Mrs. Wagner. Good to see you again."), took her keys and carefully drove the car into the club's private parking garage.

"Where's your car?" asked Julia.

"Over in the lot a couple blocks away. You didn't tell me where to park, and I've been waiting here for about fifteen minutes."

Julia's smile faded. "Traffic was heavy, and I'm sure I told you that the club would take care of the car. Too late now. Well, let's go on in," and she stopped and looked at June's footwear, dispatching an expression somewhere between horror and amusement. "June, you are wearing open-toed sandals! It's only barely May. What are you thinking?"

June looked down at her feet. "I'm thinking it's May and I would wear my new sandals today. I also thought they would be comfortable when we shop later. Why? Doesn't your club allow such things to be worn? Should I go home?"

"Don't be ridiculous," replied Julia. "I was just surprised to see them. It's not exactly sandal weather yet. Let's go on in," and the two of them entered the club where Julia stopped at the front desk and signed June in as her guest. There was a bit of a chill in the air, but it wasn't due to the air conditioning.

Julia led the way and the two were shown to their table in the club's restaurant. On the way, she stopped at two different tables to greet the women who were there. At both, she introduced June to the women as "My cousin who I thought would like to have a *nice* luncheon today." June smiled politely, but felt like the country mouse being shown the big city by her cousin, the important city mouse. She swallowed her annoyance, and reminded herself that his was to be a pleasant day. She had taken a day off work to do this, to treat herself, and she didn't want to let June spoil it. They sat down and immediately the menus were brought to them.

They quietly looked them over, and June thought she would begin the conversation politely. "Everything looks so good. I think the chicken pot pie with the side salad is what I will have. Have you had it before?"

Julia looked over at her cousin and pursed her lips. "Personally, I have not, but I understand it is good. It's rich and just a bit on the calorie-laden side for me. I'm going to have the garden salad with a bit of fresh lemon on the side. What don't you try that? It's light and refreshing. And it won't be so heavy on your stomach. Less calories too," and she smiled a smile that was not a smile.

June closed the menu and placed it to the side. She didn't explain to her cousin that if she ate the heartier chicken pot pie, she would not need to make a dinner for herself later. She had difficulty figuring out hot meals for just herself. She missed making meals for two with some left over for the following night. She missed her husband and missed talking to him over dinner and missed the fact that he told her daily she was a wonderful cook and missed…well, she just would not say anything, and would order what she wanted. She knew this was Julia's passive aggressive way of telling her she was eating too much. She would ignore her comments and suggestions.

"I'm sure the salad is light and refreshing, but I'm going to order the pot pie," and June smiled and sipped her water.

Julia shrugged. "Suit yourself. Would you like a drink? I'm going to have a martini," and she looked up as the waitress came over to take their order.

Julia ordered a martini, with two olives, and when June was asked for her preference, she said, "I'd love some hot coffee and cream," and ignored the look from her cousin. She was sure that in the club's restaurant, with some of Julia's friends around them, there would not be a comment or face made because she ordered the coffee. She hoped it was strong, and the smell carried across the table to her cousin's delicately reconstructed and just-so-slightly-tipped nose.

The drinks were brought; the coffee was delicious; the cream was real, and June happily agreed to another cup when the waitress came over. Julia had a second martini. With two olives.

They spoke about general things, unimportant things, family things, and ate their lunch. Julia drank her martinis, picked at her garden salad, and left the warm bread and whipped butter alone. June relished the delicious chicken pot pie, gathered some bread to her plate and buttered it generously. She said to her cousin, "This bread is warm and smells wonderful. Are you sure you don't want a piece? The butter is whipped. Really, Julia, you are missing out on something delicious."

Perhaps it was the two martinis (she had just ordered a third), or the smell of the coffee, or the fact that she *was* missing something delicious and was sick of the club's garden salad with fresh lemon. Was it the unimportant discussion they had been having which centered around June's children and her grandchildren, the family Julia tried not to envy, the family for which all the new red convertibles in the world could not be a substitute? Could it have been June's disgusting new sandals which Julia was sure the other club women were noticing? Might it have been the guilt that ordering the third martini brought? (Yes, there had been too many multiple martinis ordered lately.) Was it a general malaise which had consistently overcome her as she looked out across the lake through her ceiling to floor windows in the elegant, exclusive, expensive apartment in the sky, feeling a purposelessness she could not shake and which led to additional martini-ordering at the various clubs to which she belonged? Or while sitting at home alone waiting for Arnie to appear late at night? It was something; something that made her say the creatively cruel things she said to her cousin who was just finished enjoying the meal made for her at the club's lovely restaurant and was looking forward to shopping soon and spending some of the money she had saved for the occasion. What was said didn't matter. The tone, the nastiness, the malice, and bitterness did. It led to other comments. It led to ugly utterances. Both took part.

They did not raise voices. They spoke to each other in a quietness which created its own ruckus and racket, and when the waitress did come to deliver the third martini and ask about dessert (June had been thinking about the chocolate lava cake.), she left quickly with no additionally placed orders. June stood up, threw her pressed, white linen napkin on the table, gathered her purse, and without speaking again to Julia, left. She walked to her car parked in the public parking place, her new sandals clipping sharply against her bare heels, opened the driver's side door, and sat down slamming the door. For fifteen minutes, she took many cleansing breaths before she felt she could drive home safely.

Julia stayed at the table, pushed her unfinished salad to the side, and finished her third martini. She waved the waitress over, asked for and then drank two cups of hot tea, and, when done, she visited the club's expertly designed bathroom and threw up the martinis, the tea, and the few bites of garden salad with fresh lemon she had eaten. She had the front desk call for a cab explaining that she was coming down with something, and she would leave her car here but retrieve it in a couple of days. She went home to the glass building, and lay on her bed in the large bedroom. The lunch was over. No shopping was done. And they did not talk for two months.

***

There was a noise at the front door. June got up to greet her son and his new wife, and as they came into the kitchen, Deborah came out of the bedroom, closing the door softly, and the third of July family cookout officially began. Julia and June worked together to set out the rest of the appetizers, and chairs were moved about the kitchen. As they worked at serving and mixing and stirring, they laughed at the comments made and the stories shared, and a shifting of the edginess that was present occurred. It never disappeared, but the spikiness was muted, and the sawtoothed periphery assuaged.

Chapter 30   Killing

It took almost a month, and the irritability in the household remained, clouding the atmosphere, producing its own climate change. June was determined to proceed with her plan and was able to when Julia was released from physical therapy, despite her insistence that she was not completely healed.

"Mrs. Wagner," said her doctor, "the therapist said there is nothing else to be done. You are fine; your ankle is healed, and she sees no need to continue. I have examined it, and so has the orthopedic specialist you asked to be sent to. The small fracture is completely healed. In fact, it looks surprisingly good for a woman your age. Continue your walking, and do the at-home exercises you were given. We will re-check it in six months at your next regular appointment, and as always, call if you need something."

Julia was displeased with this, but there was nothing else she could say, so she nodded and, using her light oak-colored cane, she slowly went out of the office and into her car, driven by June.

"Idiots!" she barked as June pulled away. "What do they know? I'm still in pain after all these months, and everyone says I'm fine. Humph!" and she stared out the car window.

June drove for a few streets and then halted at the stoplight and waited. She made a suggestion. "We could go back to walking. That seems to be good for you, and walking up and down the staircase at the common building seemed to help you. I'll be there to watch you. Do you want to begin tomorrow?"

"I guess," and Julia created a pout with her lips, "but I will need to use this cane. Probably for the rest of my life," and she thumped it on the car floor. Twice.

June pursed her lips, glanced into the rear-view mirror, and nodded. *Probably*, she thought, *probably so*.

The next day, Thursday, the two cousins walked down the sidewalk, across the side street, and over to the front walk of the Winchester Complex common building. They went into the building's main floor where Julia rested on one of the chairs until she got her breath back. Then, using her cane to help her rise, she walked up the staircase with June behind her. She paused at the top, then came down with June in front of her, protecting her. Then after a brief rest they walked home. They made the same trip on Friday. They rested Saturday and Sunday. On Monday, they began again.

They entered the building, and Julia sat down for her rest. June looked at her and then glanced to the staircase and spoke. "I think you should be able to get up the stairs without me walking behind you. You are doing a great job. In fact, do you want to try it without your cane?"

Julia glared at her. "What an idiotic idea. No, June, my cane is necessary. Fine, I'll walk up the stairs, but where will you be?"

"I'll walk up to the top and watch you. In fact, I'll go now. When you are ready, come up the stairs."

June went to the top and stood by the banister. Eventually Julia, using her cane to assist her right ankle and holding on to the railing with her left hand, climbed up. When she got to the top, June nodded and smiled. "That was good, now come on to this side and walk down. Just be careful and go slowly." Julia moved over to the side where June was standing. She stood at the top and looked down the set of stairs. Using her cane and holding on to the railing, she ventured down. At the bottom she looked up and nodded to June who walked down the stairs. They went home.

Tuesday's walk was a success. So was Wednesday's. On Thursday, June walked up the Winchester Complex common building staircase and watched as Julia climbed to the top, walked to the other side, stood for a moment, then traveled down. June walked down after her. They went home. June was anxious all that day as she waited. Waited for Friday. Friday was the day. Friday was the day June would put her plan into action. Friday was the day she would, after months of waiting and planning and considering, kill her cousin Julia.

Chapter 31   1995 Age 65

"It's strange," commented Deborah to her brother Daniel, "that Uncle Arnie died of a heart attack suddenly just like Dad did. Don't you think so?"

"Um hum," he mumbled, and he pointed to Nancy who was holding their two-year old and motioning to him. "I better go and see what's going on with Tommy. Nancy needs me."

The funeral luncheon was being held at the club which had claimed Julia and Arnie's annual dues for almost two decades, and Julia was surrounded with a half dozen members who were attempting to comfort her. She was no longer crying, and, with the encouragement of her cousin, had even taken a few bites of the luncheon which consisted of Arnie's favorite dishes. The waiter was making his way to her, holding a tray containing her martini. She needed to fortify herself, to build up her strength to get through the remainder of the afternoon, and the hot tea she had been drinking just wasn't helping. She needed something stronger. This was a grueling time.

Arnie's death wasn't as sudden as Deborah thought it was. He appeared strong and healthy while he and Julia were on their usual yearly trip to Europe, but became unwell and increasingly frail and tired within a couple weeks of returning. Because his doctor couldn't pin-point the problem, Arnold was admitted into the hospital for some tests. He was there for two weeks, and on a Sunday evening when visiting hours were over and he was walking Julia to the elevator, he suddenly grabbed her hand, gave a lurch forward into her arms, and slid to the floor where he took his final breath. In that way, his death was sudden. Julia remained in shock, and June stayed by her side, helping to plan and organize the two-day wake, the funeral, and the refined luncheon at the club. Now it was over, and the irrevocability of it all was confirmed.

Deborah looked through the waning crowd and found her mother in a corner of the room sipping coffee and taking a needed break. She sat down next to her.

"We've said our good-byes to Aunt Julia, and Robert is going to leave with the kids and go back to your place. I thought I would stay here if I am needed, if you want me to, and we can get a cab home later. Daniel said Nancy wants to take Tommy home before he gets too crabby. This has been a long day for the kids. Robert and I plan to leave sometime tomorrow afternoon, but what do you need me to help with now?"

Her mother looked and her and smiled. Deborah saw the exhaustion in her eyes and took her mother's hand. "Mom, you should come home and rest. I'll speak to Robert, and we can arrange to stay another day or two if we are needed. We can do that. Do you think Aunt Julia will be OK?"

June pursed her lips. "No, I think she is still in shock. I packed a bag because she asked me to stay with her tonight, and I told her I would. She has a driver to take us back to her apartment, and the guests seem to be clearing out, so I think we'll leave soon. Go home with Robert and the kids, and I'll call you in the morning. Let me say good-bye to you tonight, and we'll make plans to get together in another week or so. I think I'm going to need to stay with Julia for a while. Actually, tomorrow, I'm going to try and talk her into coming to my house for a few days. I think being away from that large empty apartment might be a good thing for her. You can just close the house and lock it when you leave. It will be fine. Come on; let me say good-bye to everyone," and the two of them walked over to the front of the hall where June's family was waiting.

***

After leaving the club, the driver took the two women to the tall glass and steel building where they took the elevator to Julia's apartment. June entered the guest bedroom, put the packed overnight bag on the bed and began to remove items from it. She could hear Julia in the kitchen getting things out for tea, so she left the bag, walked there, and asked, "Can I help?"

"No; I have it done. I'm making us both some tea. The tea at the club comes in those bags and just doesn't taste as good as the Harrington's I'm used to, and I want something familiar tonight. I'm tired, but don't think I can sleep. I might take one of the pills the doctor prescribed. I'm just not sure where I put them."

"Julia, they are over to your right, behind those cups."

"Oh, yes, there they are. The tea is ready, June," and Julia brought the teapot over to the table where she poured them each a cup and sat down across from her cousin. They sipped at the hot liquid, and June didn't mention not liking tea. She thought the best action to take was to sit, drink Julia's tea, and make some normal, ordinary small-talk. She held her hands around the cup thinking that the warmth was the best part. The lights of some of the neighboring buildings were shining on the lake in the distance, and the sight made June realize this was the first time she had been in this apartment so late at night.

Julia sighed. "There are still so many things that need to be done. *Thank you* cards need to be written and sent, and I need to deal with the funeral home. I have a meeting with our lawyer in two days to go over the will and instructions left by Arnie. It will seem strange because I don't think I've ever been to our lawyer's office without Arnie. In fact, I know I haven't. June, I need you to go with me. I don't want to do this alone."

"I'll do whatever you need me to do, Julia. I'll call work in the morning and tell them I'm taking some more days off. I'm sure that won't be a problem. I've taken very few days off, and since this is my final couple of months before retiring, I'm just finishing up one or two small projects and getting things organized for the new girl. I'll need to be at work in another week when she comes in to start her training, but, sure, I can go. It will just take a phone call."

"Such changes. First Daddy and then your parents and Mama. Then Peter and Mrs. Sampson. Now Arnie. All gone. What will we do, June? What will we do?" and Julia began to cry.

June got up and moved the nearest tissue box next to Julia. She put her arm around her shoulder, patting her cousin's back, and stayed there for a bit before sitting down. She let Julia cry. June was positive this is what Doctor Spanner would have done. Allow her to grieve.

She poured more tea and threw out the used tissue and waited until Julia stopped weeping. She brought her cup to her lips to sip the tepid drink. This all seemed familiar: sitting at a table, comforting Julia, supplying tissues and tea. Julia sighed, took a swallow of the familiar Harrington's, and blew her nose.

"Really, June, what are we going to do?" she asked again.

June looked at her cousin. She had aged in the past months. Her face was drawn and pale, whatever makeup she had applied that morning had worn off, and her hair, usually so carefully coiffured was tousled, and not in a pleasant way. June caught a reflection of herself in the glass kitchen cabinet and almost laughed out loud. *I hardly look better*, she thought, *and I look my age too.* She didn't have any words to comfort Julia, any words to answer the question, any words to ease the pain, so she said the truth.

"We will continue to live, Julia. We will get up and do the tasks we need to do, and try to find some form of living, and eventually we will. I can tell you it won't be the same. There is an adjustment to make. I'm still making it. You will too. I know those may not be particularly comforting words, but it's all I have. You will go on. There's your clubs and the activities they offer, and your friends. You will keep busy."

"You don't know how it works, June. I'm a widow now. Widows aren't invited to the same get-togethers couples are. They go to fewer activities, and then there is a special table reserved for the *singles*, as they are called. That's what I am now. Oh, a few women will continue to call for a while and pretend to be interested and want to know how I'm doing, but that will stop. I know. I've done it myself. Everyone is friendly and supportive for a month or so, and then, because you are not in the same circle as you were, things will change. It happens. I've seen it. I just didn't think it would happen to me. Besides, so many of the older members are either gone or have moved to another state. People are disappearing one way or another. What will I do? What do I have to live for now? I wish my life was over too," and she began to cry again.

"Julia, you have me and the family. You have interests such as traveling, and that doesn't need to end. You have this lovely apartment in a great city and plenty to keep you busy. I know you have a subscription to the orchestra and are active in the arts. You love dining out and going to the theater and visiting museums and shopping. You will just keep up the same activities and maybe even find more things to do. Don't make any rash decisions right now because you are understandably upset. Give yourself some time."

Julia used more of the tissues and then calmed down. "How long did it take you when Peter died? When did you feel normal again?"

N*ever*, thought June. *You will never feel normal again*, but she didn't say this. "You will have changes, and there will be adjustments, and then you readjust and get used to the new things. I don't know, Julia. I don't have a timeline for you. Sorry, I don't think I'm helping you."

Her cousin sighed again and looked around at the apartment. "This place is too big. I can't imagine giving the dinner parties we used to give or entertaining the way Arnie liked to. Maybe I should move. Maybe move into one of those retirement places. Some of them are spacious and well built. Maybe we should move together somewhere. What do you think?"

June took a breath. *I think that would be awful*, she thought, but to her cousin she said, "Don't do anything quickly, Julia. Let things settle and take your time. Don't hurry into something just because you think you want an immediate change. Just ease into your changes."

The two women sat quietly for a time. The night darkened around them; the city lights faded; and a murkiness enveloped the space as they thought their separate thoughts and claimed their similar but individual solitudes.

Chapter 32   1999 Age 68+

"So, maybe move into one of those retirement places? Some of them are spacious and well built. We should move together somewhere. What do you think?"

June moved the lunch dishes to the sink, refilled her water glass and sat down across from Julia. It was Sunday, January 3, and the new year of 1999 had begun with a major blizzard which kept Julia from traveling back to her apartment. She had spent the holiday weekend with June for the third year in a row, and despite the cold and snow, a coziness was generated, produced in part by the joyful laughs and carefree yells of the neighborhood children who were out shoveling and playing, and delighting in the knowledge that their Winter Break would be extended by at least one more day due to the inclemency.

June shrugged her shoulders. "I don't know, Julia. I'm not sure about moving, and I'm unsure we would be the best roommates. This house is fine for me and has room for the kids or grandkids when they want to stay. Maybe you need to find a smaller place and would be happy somewhere else. What about moving close to some of your friends?"

"Ha! What friends? I told you when Arnie died what would happen, and it has. I have resigned from all except one of the clubs, and I'm tempted not to renew my membership to that one. I rarely go there, and when I do, so many of the older members are gone, it's just not the same. I don't know the new members who are so young. Oh, some are the children of the older members, but most of them are new and don't care to find out about or get to know the few of us left. And the friends I have left, the ones I may telephone or who call me, live in Florida, or Arizona, and a couple in California. My life has changed June. I'm tired of living in that big apartment by myself. I need to move."

"Then do it. I know your place is too large for you, and you don't entertain the way you used to. Neither do I. No one our age does. Honestly, Julia, I don't think I can afford to move. My social security and small pension just barely cover the bills here. The thought of moving and paying a new mortgage and sharing the bills isn't something I can consider. But I'll be happy to go with you and look at some places."

"OK, June, since you brought up finances, let's talk money. I have done lots of thinking and considering. I know your finances aren't what mine are. To be perfectly honest, I am quite wealthy. Between what

Daddy and Mama left me, Arnie's will, and the sale of the business, I have plenty. I want to make a suggestion, so listen."

"There isn't any need for me to listen. I can't afford to move."

"Yes, you can. If you sell this house, you can put part of it… and I mean only PART…into the new place. I can easily afford the rest. I have a terrific financial advisor, and she can help you to invest the remainder of your funds. I can afford the bills and you can cover your personal needs such as clothes, car, entertainment, any extra things you might want. In fact, you will probably be better off than being here and paying the monthly bills and upkeep on the house. Being here, in this house, you need to worry about the lawncare and snow shoveling. In a new place, that will be taken care of. I won't have any problem selling the apartment. There are always people who want to move into the building, and over the years, I have gotten several offers. I've worked it out, June. I know what I'm talking about."

"Even if the finances work out, how can I accept your offer? I can't be that indebted to you, Julia. It's not fair to you and probably not fair to me either. I can't do it."

"Let's figure this out. I can't cook or bake and you can. I'm not much of a cleaner or organizer, and you are. I will hire a cleaning service for once a month to do deep cleaning, but other than that…"

"So, I will be the live-in maid?"

Julia laughed. "Come on, June. Do you want to eat my cooking?"

"Well, let me think about this. I don't know. Where would we go? What if I wanted the kids to visit? Will there be a garage for your fancy car? I'm sure you won't want to park it on the street. What would we do there? I have friends I do things with, and I'd miss that. I'd miss my book club and exercise class, and I'm used to living in this neighborhood."

Julia reached into her large purse and pulled out some pamphlets. She pushed them over to June. "Take a look at these. I've been to some places already, and have narrowed it down to this one. I did some traveling last fall, and looked around. This is a great place. It's in one of the western suburbs, and is specifically for people our age. It's called the *Winchester Senior Complex*, and once this awful weather clears, we should take a ride there and look around. When I was there, they were building new housing, and one of the models was a townhouse which seemed perfect for us."

"You seem to have this all figured out."

"I do. I do have it figured out. There is a two-car garage and three bedrooms with two baths. One for each of us. Guests can stay in the third bedroom, and there is a lovely deck on the back which looks out over the yard. Of course, you'll need to get rid of these indoor plants you insist on. They aggravate my allergies. There will be plenty of outdoor trees and flowers for you. The owners are putting in a man-made lake with a walking path. And there's nothing we will need to do for upkeep. The complex takes care of the yard and snow, and we aren't that far from the town which contains restaurants and shops. In fact, I had lunch at a lovely place and bought a new outfit at one of the shops there. Remember the yellow-striped one I wore last summer? Anyway, it will be perfect for us."

"Julia, stop. There are too many things to think about. I just don't know. I am so used to this house and to living here. I'll still miss the activities I enjoy doing."

"And that's taken care of too. There's a common area that has an exercise room, and there are many things planned all the time. Wait, one of those sheets is a schedule for the activities for last October, but you can see the kinds of things that are scheduled. Let me see where it is," And Julia reached over to pull the sheets and pamphlets back and shuffled through them.

June reached over and put her hand on top of them. "Stop. I'll look through these. I promise. I'll find the activity sheet. I just don't know, Julia. You seem to have made a decision, and there are so many things I need to consider. I'll need to go over the information for myself, and talk to Deborah and Daniel, and think through the finances. Moving is a big endeavor, and selling this house would be painful. I have come to love it here, and to really like my neighbors. You are moving too fast. Give me some time to think it through, and once the weather is better, in a couple months, we can take a ride there. But don't hurry me."

"Fine. Look everything over, and think about it. Really, June, I've thought through this whole thing, but I waited to say something to you until the time was right. It's right. This would be good for both of us. Remember when we were girls and spent all those weekends together? We had fun, and it could be like that again. Think about it. Soon we'll be sixty-nine years old, and by the time we're seventy, we could be in a new place and celebrate the beginning of the new millennium together. It will be great!"

"Well, we were young and times were different. How do you know we'll be good roommates? We are older adults and set in our ways. We have both changed over the years and are different people now. How do you know we'll even get along, Julia?"

"Don't be silly, June. Of course we will. We'll be fine. It will be delightful to live together. We have so much in common and know each other so well. It will all work out. You'll see. After all, we're almost sisters! I'm looking forward to being roommates!"

"Hmm," mumbled June to herself as she picked up the first pamphlet and began to examine the pictures inside.

ANNOUNCING A NEW STATE-OF-THE-ART SENIOR COMPLEX

Chapter 33   Friday
The First Last Chapter

Friday. The early spring weather was delicious. A soft breeze blew, but was not strong enough to mess one's hair. A short, light spring jacket was needed, but by noon, a light sweater would do. Graceful wispy flowers peeked out of the ground, and if one looked closely, a small leaf bud or two could be observed on the trees. It was a perfect day. A perfect day for a killing.

June drank no coffee that morning. She wanted no caffeine to distract her clear thinking. She prepared Julia's usual tea thinking this may very well be the final time for the task. She set the table and made the oatmeal hoping that the next time she would only need to prepare one serving. She could only eat a couple spoonsful, but she watched as her cousin ate with her usual hearty appetite. Then she began to have second thoughts.

What was she doing? Did Julia deserve this? Was there something wrong with her thinking about ~~killing~~ subduing Julia? As Julia watched her usual morning television and sipped her tea, June reviewed the *Pro/Con* list she created in her head months ago. Had anything changed? No. Everything remained the same. Maybe she should rethink things anyway. Perhaps she hadn't given Julia enough credit. Perhaps she would become civil and kind. Maybe June hadn't given her enough time. Enough understanding. Enough attention.

"HEY," yelled Julia, "Are you paying attention to me? I asked you twice for more lemons. Really, June, you are such a dolt," and she shook her head and turned the sound up on the television.

June got up to cut additional lemon slices. She cut them with renewed resolve and placed them on the table for her cousin.

Julia poured and assembled another cup of tea and said, "I'm going to finish my program in the front room while you clean up. Then we can walk. Afterwards I think I'll take a nap. I'm tired today. Didn't sleep well last night. Whatever you were doing in the kitchen kept me up. You need to be more considerate, June," and Julia walked into the front room. Without her cane.

June did not answer her. She cleaned the breakfast dishes, put everything away, and sat down at the table to think. She thought back to the past months, to her deciding, justifying, doubting, hoping, readjusting, reassessing, planning, delaying, changing, waiting, devising, resolving, and now the killing. Friday: the day for the killing. She glanced at the kitchen clock and saw that the morning programs were done. She put on her short, light spring jacket and picked up Julia's cane to take to her. She passed Julia's bedroom and saw she was getting her own short, light spring jacket on.

She handed her the cane, saying nothing, and the two cousins walked out of the house they shared, down the sidewalk, across the side streets, and over to the front walk of the Winchester Complex common building. They went into the building's main floor, and Julia rested on one of the chairs until she got her breath back. June went to the top and stood by the banister. Eventually Julia, using her cane to assist her right ankle and holding on to the railing with her left hand, climbed up. When she got to the top, June nodded and smiled. "That was good, now come on to this side and walk down." Julia moved over. She stood at the top and looked down the set of stairs.

There was a microscopic moment of hesitation. A meager nanosecond of pause. A piddling point during which June had her chance to do the thing she planned to do for months. To take revenge, to make things proper, to settle scores, to kill her cousin Julia. All she had to do was to move her foot forward and gently tap the light oak-colored cane with her toe. The cane Julia was leaning on. The one that was partly off the top landing. One unobtrusive, unpretentious, unimportant movement and Julia would go tumbling down the stairs, rolling and somersaulting and plummeting to an absolute fatal *thunk* at the bottom of the flight of stairs in the main building of the Winchester Senior Complex. An accident. An atrocious, horrifying regular accident. June took a deep cleansing breath.

***

And then she stepped back one tiny pace.

Julia placed her left hand on the railing and walked down the stairs, waiting at the bottom for June to follow her. June walked down. At the bottom, Julia turned to June and smiled, "That was fine. You know, I think on Monday I will begin to walk without a cane. I really do feel better today. Maybe it's the spring weather or the fact that the contestants on the show this morning weren't so stupid. Anyway, let's get home. You can make me more tea. Come on, slowpoke."

Julia pushed open the front door of the Winchester Senior Complex. Her light spring jacket was almost too warm, and when the two cousins got back to the townhouse they shared, she would hang it up, mentioning again to June that the weather was turning; spring was arriving; the day seemed promising.

June followed her out the front door. They walked together down the street, and Julia arranging herself so that she could hook her right arm through June's left arm. She held the cane in her left hand, unused. June sighed quietly. Then she took a cleansing breath. And then she took two more. They walked together. In the spring weather, with a slight breeze blowing, but not strong enough to mess one's hair, June, with her companion's arm tightly anchored to hers, walked to the townhouse she would continue to share with her cousin Julia.

Chapter 34   Friday
The Second Last Chapter

Friday. The early spring weather was delicious. A soft breeze blew, but was not strong enough to mess one's hair. A short, light spring jacket was needed, but by noon, a light sweater would do. Graceful wispy flowers peeked out of the ground, and if one looked closely, a small leaf bud or two could be observed on the trees. It was a perfect day. A perfect day for a killing.

June drank no coffee that morning. She wanted no caffeine to distract her clear thinking. She prepared Julia's usual tea thinking this may very well be the final time for the task. She set the table and made the oatmeal hoping that the next time she would only need to prepare one serving. She could only eat a couple spoonsful, but she watched as her cousin ate with her usual hearty appetite. Then she began to have second thoughts.

What was she doing? Did Julia deserve this? Was there something wrong with her thinking about ~~killing~~ subduing Julia? As Julia watched her usual morning television and sipped her tea, June reviewed the *Pro/Con* list she created in her head months ago. Had anything changed? No. Everything remained the same. Maybe she should rethink things anyway. Perhaps she hadn't given Julia enough credit. Perhaps she would become civil and kind. Maybe June hadn't given her enough time. Enough understanding. Enough attention.

"HEY," yelled Julia, "Are you paying attention to me? I asked you twice for more lemons. Really, June, you are such a dolt," and she shook her head and turned the sound up on the television.

June got up to cut additional lemon slices. She cut them with renewed resolve and placed them on the table for her cousin.

Julia poured and assembled another cup of tea and said, "I'm going to finish my program in the front room while you clean up. Then we can walk. Afterwards I think I'll take a nap. I'm tired today. Didn't sleep well last night. Whatever you were doing in the kitchen kept me up. You need to be more considerate, June," and Julia walked into the front room. Without her cane.

June did not answer her. She cleaned the breakfast dishes, put everything away, and sat down at the table to think. She thought back to the past months, to her deciding, justifying, doubting, hoping, readjusting, reassessing, planning, delaying, changing, waiting, devising, resolving, and now the killing. Friday: the day for the killing. She glanced at the kitchen clock and saw that the morning programs were done. She put on her short, light spring jacket and picked up Julia's cane to take to her. She passed Julia's bedroom and saw she was getting her own short, light spring jacket on.

She handed her the cane, saying nothing, and the two cousins walked out of the house they shared, down the sidewalk, across the side streets, and over to the front walk of the Winchester Complex common building. They went into the building's main floor, and Julia rested on one of the chairs until she got her breath back. June went to the top and stood by the banister. Eventually Julia, using her cane to assist her right ankle and holding on to the railing with her left hand, climbed up. When she got to the top, June nodded and smiled. "That was good, now come on to this side and walk down." Julia moved over. She stood at the top and looked down the set of stairs.

There was a microscopic moment of hesitation. A meager nanosecond of pause. A piddling point during which June had her chance to do the thing she planned to do for months. To take revenge, to make things proper, to settle scores, to kill her cousin Julia. All she had to do was to move her foot forward and gently tap the light oak-colored cane with her toe. The cane Julia was leaning on. The one that was partly off the top landing. One unobtrusive, unpretentious, unimportant movement and Julia would go tumbling down the stairs, rolling and somersaulting and plummeting to an absolute fatal *thunk* at the bottom of the flight of stairs in the main building of the Winchester Senior Complex. An accident. An atrocious, horrifying regular accident. June took a deep cleansing breath.

***

And then she inched forward one imperceptible pace and nudged the cane which was partly off the top landing with the tip of her left toe.

Julia's face turned a pale shade of white. She leaned forward to grab the cane which was just out of her reach. As it clucked down the steps like an amateur acrobat, Julia followed. She attempted to grab the savior railing, but was unable to manage it, and her fingers, moving through the air, suggested she was completing those finger exercises for the piano which she refused to do as a child. She left out a scream which sounded like, "NOOOWAITTTWHATTTHEEELLPPPP," which was mixed with June's scream of, "Jjuulliiaa!!!", a noise she didn't know she was going to make. It hadn't been in her plan. She hadn't thought what she would do or say after the deed had been done. Later, as she sat at her kitchen table, Alice sitting next to her, she thought she remembered screaming, "Soorrrryyy!!!" but wasn't certain.

There were nauseating reverberations as Julia's head hit one step and then another and one leg flew up in the air and smacked down on the railing and then on the stair, and Julia's arms swam continually in wild forward strokes, hoping to find assistance and support, and scarlet streams of liquid began to appear on various parts of Julia's body, and her short light spring jacket became tangled beneath her as she rolled and lurched and toppled to the bottom of the stairs, her head landing on her light-colored oak cane which was waiting for her at the bottom and which gave Julia's skull a finishing beating as she finally and fatally came to a stop. A decisive and definitive stop. The ultimate end to an appalling, gruesome, shocking, regular accident.

***

After the shouting and the screaming and the calling and the ambulancing and the reporting; after the somberness and hopelessness and discreetness; after the phoning and arranging and preparing, June was taken home by her friend, Alice, who sat in the kitchen with her, keeping her company, and providing comfort and tissues as June cried. She cried for many reasons, but Alice ministered to her, and assured her, and helped her assemble and organize what would be a grave and gloomy week. Alice got June calmed down and offered to stay with her a few nights. Wes wouldn't mind, and June needed someone until her daughter, Deborah, arrived. Finally, June was soothed. She was wholly appreciative of Alice's efforts. And when Alice asked if she would like some coffee, June perked up and smiled.

"Thanks, Alice, coffee would be perfect. I enjoy the smell as much as the taste. Some coffee would be great."

Alice pulled out the new old coffee pot and began to measure the coffee grounds and water. As they waited for the coffee, she looked over to the corner where the unopened box containing the new single cup coffee maker, the gift from Julia, rested. "Why, June, I didn't know you had one of these. Is it new? Have you used it yet?"

"Not yet," replied June looking at the new coffee maker with fondness, "I don't have the coffee capsules for it. When Deborah gets here, we'll shop for some, and she can show me how to use it. She has one at her house."

Alice nodded. She opened the refrigerator and took out the creamer; she picked up the freshly made pot of coffee; she poured them both a steaming cup of the dark and welcoming liquid and sat down. The two friends, privately reveling in the advent of the vernal season, sipped the coffee, savoring the smell and the taste; enjoying the warmth and amiability and contentment it provided. Outside, the gentle spring breeze, not enough to mess one's hair, pushed against the wispy flowers peeking out of the ground causing them to sway in their space. Inside, the two women sat at the kitchen table, talking, discussing, and determining what June's life would be like now. Now that she was on her own. Now that she would be alone in the house. Now that June was completely autonomous, totally solitary, absolutely and entirely self-sufficient. Now that June was no longer living with her cousin Julia.

Read an excerpt from

Susan M. Szurek's

next book:

My Brother's Things

Excerpt from *My Brother's Things*

The Box

Even though I expected the box to arrive, I was surprised, as I parked in the driveway after work, to see it resting on my front porch. It had been some time since Steve and I drove to Indiana to take care of my brother and arrange for his cremation. My brother is currently sitting on the upper shelf of my closet, waiting for me to do something permanent with him. I haven't decided what yet.

Steve and I traveled to South Bend during the last days of the summer break. A week later, when we returned, tasks awaited us. There was a hurried school shopping trip for the kids, my unfinished preparation for the new high school history class I was to teach in the fall, and my mother-in-law's insistence that her son finish the restoration of her dining room table and chairs he had promised to complete for her birthday. Our kitchen was only half painted, the old oven needed replacing, the tomatoes in the vegetable garden were overripe, and it all needed immediate attention. The kitchen is still unfinished. So, the box, when it arrived, was simply another task for me to undertake, and I was not ready for it.

I went into the house through the garage door, placed my purse and bookbag on the kitchen table, gave a brief thought as to what dinner would be, and opened the front door where the box was waiting. I glanced at the return address. It was from the hospital in Indiana. We were told that when my brother was admitted, his leather duffle bag was on the ambulance gurney with him, but it was removed. It was taken, labeled, and placed in a storage area. Due to the complications about the accident and his subsequent death, it was forgotten when we arrived. A week or so after returning home, I received a phone call from someone there and was told that as soon as possible the bag would be boxed and sent to me, and I promptly forgot about it. And here it was. On the front porch.

It wasn't heavy or even large, but it was awkward. I dragged it into the front hallway and stood up. I was not ready to delve into this mystery. I didn't know what items were in it, but I knew it would take more than a cursory glance, and I was not mentally prepared for it yet. The box needed to be put away. I didn't need either of my teenagers coming home from school and wanting to dig into it. It was none of their business, and I was not sure what I would find. I opened the front closet and looked for a space. Towards the back, on the floor there was a large basket containing winter boots. Pulling it out, I realized that they would need to be reorganized and some replaced. Jim was a senior and his feet were large. He would never fit into the boots that were there, and Kate wouldn't fit into hers either, although I suspected it was more of a style rejection than a size issue. There were some other boots which were mine and some I didn't recognize, and before winter the entire basket needed to be tended to. But not today.

As I pulled out the boots to create a space and shoved the box into it, I wondered if I should drag it upstairs to my closet and allow these things to rest with the owner. But time was getting away, and in another few minutes, the two would return and see this. I could hear them asking, "Is this for me/us?", "Can we open it?", "What's in it?" *No, no,* and *I don't know* would be the answers, and I wasn't prepared to deal with it now. I knew I would need some time when I was able to be solitary, to open the box, to look through the duffle bag which was I knew was inside, to view what remained of my brother's life, and while secluded in my room, to confront my brother's things.

My Brother

My brother was ten when I was born; fifteen when I was five, and twenty when I was ten. I have some memories of him: helping me learn to ride a bike, teaching me to play chess, teasing me when a boy I liked showed up at the house to sit on the porch with me. The gap in our ages meant we never completely knew each other, and by the time I was twelve, he was twenty-two, grown, and gone. He was the one person in my life, the only person, I never really knew.

When he left, I didn't know where he went. Our parents never spoke about him in front of me, although I would hear his name as they spoke to each other in the kitchen or front room, ending their conversation when I appeared. Before he left, he and Dad would argue. They would go out by the back fence, away from the house, and talk in voices which became increasingly louder. During these times, Mom would be in the kitchen, pretending to complete tasks while watching the two of them through the kitchen window. Sometimes their discussions were short, fifteen minutes or so, but often they went on for over an hour, and as their voices got louder, Mom would walk out to the back porch and stand there, then move down to the grass, and quietly take another step closer, threatening them with her presence, with her sixty-two inches of motherliness and accelerating worry. Once they noticed her stealthy approach, they would end the talk, and Dad would walk into the house, past Mom, past me, into the front room where he would turn on the television and stare at it for the next hour. My brother would disappear. Sometimes he would be gone for an hour or two. Other times, for a day or two. I never knew what their arguments were about. I was young and didn't realize then the consequences of passionate discourse.

After high school, my brother attended a nearby college, living there, sharing an apartment with other students. He worked part-time, and during academic breaks, would come home for the family dinners although he rarely stayed more than a couple days. Much of that time he would be in his room playing the drum set that was shoved into the corner or plunking his guitar. He and Dad tried, for Mom's sake, to get along, but those times, those dinners, were filled with spiky edges. After some years of half-hearted education, his roommates left or graduated, and he came home for a week, piling some ragged furniture, the old guitar, and bags of kitchen utensils in the corner of the garage. He would sit in his room or poke around the hood of his old car, and when he wasn't doing that, he stayed in his room making lengthy phone calls to people I didn't know. I heard him talk to Jack or Tommy or Bud, but those were not the names of his previous roommates, and I didn't know any of his friends. Mom tried to talk to him about his future, about his plans and possible jobs, and asked about a future with his current girlfriend, but he just said they had broken up, and he didn't know what he was going to do. Dad would come home from work and look at my brother and shake his head, and they would often engage in one of their talks which led to an uncomfortable evening for all of us.

Eventually, my brother disappeared. I should have realized he was going somewhere. He began to sell his things. Some teenagers came to the house and he helped them carry his drum set to their car. Then the old furniture from the garage disappeared, and his guitar was gone. One day he got into his car, left, and came back on a motorcycle which he worked on for a few days. On my twelfth birthday, after dinner and singing and cake, my brother gave me a bracelet which just fit on my wrist and which I still have. He kissed my head and whispered, "To remember me," and the following morning as the birthday balloons which had decorated the dining room wall for my celebration were found on the floor, the air easing out of them, the motorcycle was gone. So was my brother. He left a note. In his loopy handwriting he wrote:

Don't worry about me. I'll be fine. I'll stay in touch.

Underneath the pithy note was scrawled a large artistic *J*. That was his signature.

Jonathan.

Jab.

***

CPSIA information can be obtained
at www.ICGtesting.com
Printed in the USA
LVHW082054161122
733364LV00030B/331

9 781957 169194